Tuko's Cave

By Fritz Blackburn

Contents

Going inside and looking out

The very old woman took Tuko's hand and led him to the Tree, the shaded place where the elders, surrounded by toddlers, infants, and babe-carrying mothers usually spent the heat of day. Now, there was nobody, except for the pig tied to a nearby sapling, eagerly awaiting the wrung-out grated coconut that it knew was coming, and the rooster, for once quiet, occupied with something small and wriggly. Still holding his hand with her dry, strongly wrinkled, bony fingers, Narra, the old Mananambal, stood and looked deep into Tuko's eyes for a long, challenging moment. It did not make him uncomfortable. Her eyes may have been like stones falling through space, but there was a twinkle of profound understanding as well as that Filipina warmth, aged to authentic sweetness. "I know what you seek, young man!" She squeezed his hand and smiled, cracking every line and wrinkle in her face, arranging them into fascinating new patterns of benevolent wisdom. "You are ready; you know? Only few ask those questions you ask, and not with your passion! You got everybody talking about animals having a soul, and plants being intelligent, and babies choosing their parents. You want to know truth. About God, the universe, about yourself? Yes, you are ready!"

She placed a banana-leaf wrapped parcel on the split bamboo deck that neatly surrounded the Tree, and slowly unfolded its content. There were twenty-five gray mushrooms with a few purple smudges. "Do not take lunch, Tuko, you already had breakfast! Take these mushrooms with you to the cave my great grandson Joel will show you and eat them there. Eat nothing else! There is water in the cave. Spend the night in the cave and come back tomorrow!"

Tuko had learned to respect the old sorceress in the time he stayed with this family that lived a good walk inland from Bulalacao. Everybody respected and adored her. She always knew exactly what she was doing. He had seen her heal a child just by touching. He had no doubt she knew what she was doing now, so he accepted the cool parcel and without words touched his forehead with the wrinkled hand that had given it. The old woman kissed his forehead, loudly calling "Joel" across to the coconut-tree studded slope where young boys were trying to ride an adult-sized bicycle between the trees and a few astonished watching water buffaloes. "Don't take anything except a warm shirt, long trousers, and your water bottle," added the Mananambal, turning away from the little boy that was about to arrive. "You may get answers to all your questions tonight! And if you get scared—breathe! Breathing is the key, don't forget that!" The boy was keen to be on their way, so Tuko went to his hut, dressed, and grabbed his drinking bottle, clicked it to his belt. They soon had left the inhabited area behind and followed a near invisible goat path through the steaming jungle. Lunch-time over, the afternoon shaped up to make for another blistering hot day. After spending weeks on the glorious beaches of Puerto Galera and then Bulalacao, swimming for hours every day, having glorious sex with a Goddess on one of the smaller islands, the effort of a hard walk up the mountain path quickly caused a good sweat. They did however more or less follow a gurgling little stream that held good, cool water to freshen up with occasionally. The trees eventually broke to take them to a clearing where the water cascaded down in a stepped waterfall from a high wall of glittering rock. Dragon-flies flirted with the spray and there were several types of butterfly Tuko had not seen before, dancing in chaotic harmony between flowering plants along the water. *Surely*, he suddenly thought, *beauty must be at the heart of what is true, at the core of all understanding.*

"Where you from, sir?" Joel had been quiet while walking, but now he sat down on a rock, looking interested. "From a little village near Admont in Austria, Joel, and you, sir?" "Oh, oh, I'm from here," Joel stated the obvious. "Why do you spend the night in the cave, sir? Are you not afraid?" Tuko laughed but was then serious with his answer. "Joel, we hear so many voices with our ears and see so many pictures with our eyes. Where can you find enough quiet to get far enough away from the noise and distraction? To find out about yourself and about God, and about how you feel inside when you are alone." Joel looked as if this made complete sense to him. "You can see the cave from here!" He pointed to a tree high up above the clearing. "Behind that tree! Easy to find, only follow the back of this hill. I will leave you now. Me very hungry!" "Bye, and thank you for bringing me here, Joel," said Tuko, feeling his own first pangs of appetite. In a blink, the boy disappeared in the forest, and then there was just the humming of insects, the clicking sounds of the dragon-flies changing gears, and the voice of water falling and jumping between stones. Another perfect paradise! How could anybody feel alone surrounded by so much amazing life? Tuko stripped naked, walked into the pool underneath the fall and took a shower that left him clean and ready for the final climb to the cave. Dried by the sun in minutes, he soon hiked up the slope, climbing over boulders and across a crevasse seamed with pink little flowers, and past a few massive old trees, until he found the right tree. The cave mouth behind it was large enough to comfortably walk in, although the cave-floor near the entrance looked a bit uneven and a little wet. A snake had been lying there on a hot rock, and now it slithered downwards into the cave and disappeared. "Great," Tuko said out loud. It was a New Moon, and he had no torch. Think positive! *Snakes don't bite calm people!* He took out the banana-leaf parcel and proceeded to eat the clean enough fungi he had been given by the sorceress. Their slightly acidic taste brought back the boy's question—was he scared? What should he be scared about? The truth? Unknown fears? Ghosts? Snakes may be. No, he was ready to face whatever came up, he had nothing to hide from himself, no discomfort to run from. Maybe he *was* ready! Maybe this was exactly what he most needed. So, he carefully climbed down the mouth of the cave and found a dry, vaulted room with an almost even floor, as well as a smaller grotto that adjoined where a trickle of water ran down a ledge that it had carved into the wall. He refilled the water bottle and climbed back outside to check for the snake but saw a red fireball of sun visibly fall toward the treeline, reminding him how short the days here were. The cooling air and the buzzing of several mosquitoes reminded Tuko to put on his shirt and track-pants. Then he smacked two of the suckers that landed on his semi-exposed wrist.

His two years of study at the "Institut für Physik" in Graz seemed far behind him in the past now; not quite real when compared to being a *part* of nature, and to *feeling* how things worked. The swimming had washed off much of the academic dust, and the Filipino smiles had warmed his receptive heart, softened the warrior athlete and given him back his boyhood sense of adventure. Life was precious and it was *now*. And without a doubt he was in paradise!

Quickly spreading shadows had Tuko furtively looking around for snakes, but there was nothing—only the yawning mouth of the cave that now vaguely looked like the vagina of a large, black woman, the tree one of her shamelessly pulled up legs, a cluster of piled boulders the other. When he entered, an earthy acidity was in his mouth and a sense of knowing himself with purpose, with immediacy, endowed with near ritual-like significance. He felt like nothing was ever going to be the same again...

He was drawn to a spot where he sat down after brushing off the bat dung that seemed to hang everywhere, and a rounded part of the cave-wall offered lower back support when he leaned back slightly. It was now completely dark. The only thing that connected him with the world was the touch of the rock-wall, and the smell of guano. The bats must have flown out already, if there were still any. And there was the snake somewhere, but he heard nothing, not even the water, from where he sat. The world had disappeared.

The cave seemed to amplify the silence, throwing it all back at him from its rounded walls, an orchestra of non-music, almost too loud for its intense non-substance. And the dark cave was—breathing! It was like a living thing, a belly that digested sounds and images, breaking them up into their composite parts, only to release them rearranged into something beyond themselves. The same was true for thoughts and emotions. Thoughts were loud things that the cave would not ignore or tolerate without exposing them exactly for what they were. Most were too silly to even entertain, and, of course, the snake also was unlikely to accept casual or merit-less thoughts...But the darkness also held a different sort of significance that could not be escaped so easily. The black walls hid long-forgotten images of early childhood that spoke of forgotten pain, of undigested realities, of fearful experiences—and there was no way to avoid, to walk away from any of it! Tuko felt instantly sick enough to vomit as soon as he tried to avoid what *was*. But as soon as he embraced what the cave put to him—the fearful energy instantly evaporated, and he soon saw with new eyes what was going on. There was no running from the truth here, that much he understood. There were images of death and dying, prenatal images, memories of birth, and they all held a potential of fear that he was sure could be faced to then be released by the cave. There was no other way to reach well-being. Every feeling and every thought instantly projected themselves in full color and unforgiving sound onto the canvas of absolute darkness, but things that he could accept no longer received any energy and faded out. Tuko knew that whatever happened from here on would be his creation alone. For now—*he* was the creator, and he was his only hope. He was quite possibly all there was, all there could be.

What was he doing here? Why was he here? Oh yeah—to discover Truth, that was it. Of course!

Who was he and why was he? Was he one to want the truth given to him casually? Did he expect to get the truth for free, or by luck? By thinking? Things were not like that, no. He would have to do the actual work he now knew was waiting for him, the work needed to be ready for ultimate truth. And not some time in the future. Now! There was no other time—and there never had been! Only a full personal commitment to now and here could possibly go further than this...this mix of reality and illusion, this entrapment by age, gender, upbringing, genes, culture and religious teachings everybody identified as reality. The entrapment by the body. All these factors precluded the mind from simply perceiving what there really *was*. Another trap was obviously greed, even the greed for knowledge or truth! Greed was too active-minded to retain the ability to receive, too focused on one thing to allow circumspection and wholeness of perspective. As soon as he had a handle on these insights, he started breathing out his greed for knowledge, emptying himself of desire of all kinds, one breath for all the forms desire took for him. This worked so perfectly well that he did the same thing for fear and anger and every other bad attitude he found in himself. The strange thing was—he knew with complete certainty that what he was doing here was exactly *it*, was the best possible shortcut through the tasks he felt he had to face. It was like having a finger on the pulse of reality and of self-creation! The more he simply and honestly looked at himself, the clearer everything became. The act of thinking became very slow and there was no 'doing' in it now. And the thoughts he started having felt sacred, eternal even, as if not at all his own.

Tuko became increasingly aware of his body losing its former solidity and mixing its substance with its surroundings, like an ethereal thing that, freed from the illusions of the eye, proved to be nothing but pure energy. Where was he—and where began the rock, the air? Was it all in one piece, as it seemed to him in the dark? Another wave of incense-like sacredness flooded every thought with natural magic, and Tuko no longer saw himself as one of six billion people, his mind only one of many. In the here and now, all reference to other humans was now gone, irrelevant! There was only himself, an archaic man, and only him. He was the One here, now. Maybe there was only the One—and he was the only fully conscious part of it...

A strong fragrance of the eternally sacred transported his senses into fuller acceptance, into fuller *responsibility*. Frankincense? The smell of earth? He filled himself with it. The cave walls felt as if they were leaning down on him in embrace or ownership; he could feel their touch on his skin, like neurons of awareness growing on the outside of his body. From all directions, living earth spirits reached out to him and whispered of death and decay, but only those things actually died that he did not wish to retain. Illusions mostly, ego, and fear of death disintegrated with every impeccable breath. *They were all teachers, those spirits!* With this, his body expanded towards the cave walls, until he felt himself filling up the entire cave, until he sat packed in a cave that felt like a tight-fitting garment. Where did *he* end, and where did the cave begin? To think this made him laugh out loud! Those defined borders between things were nothing but illusion based on imagined division! He inhaled what was *outside*, and gave back to the air what he had only just held deep *inside*. Had he not always eaten the outside, making it his inside and his own substance, and then shat it all back to the outside—just as his body itself would eventually decay and return to the 'outside,' the earth? A cyclical race from mother earth, back to mother earth—that was his body! A moment in the life of earth. He knew with suddenly brilliant clarity that he, Tuko, *was* earth! A participant of earth, a flicker of *her* life, her awareness.

Moisture trickled with intimate scents from rocky crevices and hidden nooks over smooth stony surfaces, changing into inner juices that seeped on, through the membranes and canals of the cave, through the body that also was the cave. His body was truly *the* cave he inhabited. He had always lived inside a cave! Quite different from a look into the mirror and seeing himself from the outside, as a shape! He sat inside a dark cave that was his body! There was no way out, no exit for his incarnated soul! Humans can see mountains far more easily than caves, and they perceive things and bodies only ever from the outside, as a surface, and know therefore little about what things really *are.* Humans look from the inside out, but rarely from the outside in. Some Tibetan monks might...But now it was suddenly quite possible to look inside of things, like the stomach, the liver, Tuko realized, and did just that. The liver was simply another such cave, where he could sit inside and wonder where he was and what he was doing. A cave in a cave in a cave. There could not be any one 'real' cave, only a place where his attention was at the time. Reality just followed attention, and was created by attention. From inside his liver, the universe looked not so much different—but all the rules were changed! Every cave had its own rules...

His individual cells as well were such caves into which he could fit his awareness, where familiar juices flowed and where his spirit found a home vast enough for comfort. Galaxies of even smaller particles offered a journey into still smaller caves, but he felt too thick to try entering one. They were more electric than solid to his taste. He noticed something though, when watching those moving little things—the galaxies of tiny objects *changed* their structure depending on feelings that accompanied his awareness! His thoughts and emotions actually ruled the pattern of those little worlds, created them, and destroyed them! Anger created galaxies of adrenalin compounds that were tiny worlds that had not existed before the emotion created them. Happy thoughts also produced new worlds, dopamine galaxies and oxytocin planets maybe. Worlds full of life, as it felt to him. What incredible power his attention had in those smaller caves inside! It was godlike! Every thought was an act of creation, an irrevocable change of history for these inner worlds...*He* was their universe!

Mostly however, his body was empty space... The tiny rest—whirling galaxies of tiny worlds, of caves—if one bothered to look inside. Were all these tiny worlds empty, dead? Or were there also little observers standing on their surfaces or sitting inside their caves, like himself, asking questions like—*what* is the universe? What do those stars mean, that arise in the morning, and set at night? Electrons, stars—such circling lights existed on each one of the inner worlds inside his body! And he was their universe, the whole of it.

He put his hands onto the rock behind him and instantly became aware that even this hard stone was empty space, containing tiny caves that rotated at incredible speeds. He was elbow deep into the rock and pulled back his hands in astonished wonder. He was still mixed up with everything else...flying at near speed of light! To calm himself he concentrated on the empty space that was most of himself, the darkness. But the more he looked at the nothing—the more all the stars began to twinkle and the little caves glowed each in their own subtle light, a blue sapphire-like haze replacing the dark. The darkness and the emptiness were an illusion, an invitation to discover the treasures of the deep. Fullness was the truth behind emptiness. Something in the universe opened...

Only moments ago, temples of silence—the luminescent caves now vibrated like living crystals, resonating and harmonizing with each other to some kind of common beat, like an orchestra that had always played, but never been heard before. And every little voice connected with a memory, an emotional content, like a sunken chord of long-forgotten music in a vast ocean, or thousands of didgeridoos whispering about death and infinity. From inside and out, the earth now raised her booming voice, and from every grotto of the night it wafted like an ancient call, wrapped in a holy fragrance—it was hard to say which one—and things emerged breathing from ancient graves, filling the belly of the universe with their un-ended life. Yes, everything was totally alive, Tuko saw that now. Everything! All the little worlds inside his body were alive! Of course, they were—they were parts of him, a living thing. All the atomic systems that made up his body-cells, those racing electrons, the heavy protons, the empty space—all of that was alive! He wondered how many, even space-traveling, civilizations might exist on the surfaces of those trillions of tiny worlds inside his body, that were in themselves living things. The atomic system was like a little solar system indeed...He began to see crazy things now, that he could not take in without some discomfort. Tuko continued to concentrate on breathing to regain clarity, but immediately the breathing drew him in even deeper. It had to do with letting himself *be breathed*, just watching it like a witness, and with the right posture...He felt his energy traveling up his spine, tickling the bone at the top of his skull—then running over his face, through his tongue, down the front of his body much like a warm and erotic waterfall. Tuko just went with it for a long time, concentrating only on breathing, but aware of his inner universe, of the never imagined glory of it.

And the humility! Just as surely as he was the complete universe for all those inner worlds—he was also a tiny part himself within a much larger universe. The outer universe, or macrocosm, that people meant when talking of 'space', was as equally alive and as equally complete as himself! He had lost concentration. Back to breathing. This was too much! Breathe...

Take it easy, just breathe...He watched particles made up of three forces, always three, with various spin and temperament. All things were made up of three, *all* things, which reminded him strangely of the Celtic sun-cult that asserted the number of the sun and of creation to be three. The name the world gave to this, he now remembered, was 'quark.' At home, Tuko ate quark in cheesecake! That made him laugh, and the sound of it did not disturb him this time, nor did anything else here really mind. It only produced new galaxies of good in his body. He laughed some more when he thought of how superficially the world looked at reality: an apple, for instance, is utterly invisible to humans, as they see only that side of the surface of that apple they face at that time—not the other side, not any of its inner spaces, be it cells, atoms, molecules, or just the seeds. Even those colors that define half of what humans can see—were optical illusions, rather than actual reality. Only the most external shape is discernible to the ordinary mind as an apple, which allows for no more than the vaguest guesswork about the actual reality of an apple. All people can see is a play of light and shape, depending on their position. Most still believed that matter was solid, as they could not face the fact that all was energy, and over 99,99% percent of it all—empty space... The way people, including the scientists, saw reality told much more about their own peculiar way of looking, about their methods and technical limitations, their particular interests and even their size, than it ever did give any clue about the true reality of the observed object. Because of the size difference, the scientists saw those tiny worlds as 'dead', or as 'probability waves', the location of which could not even be determined. Objective science looked from a fixed position that saw nothing more of microcosmic life than an ant on Alpha Centauri would see of Earth. It takes a very subjective science to travel where no instrument can go—and arrive back with personal knowledge that is then hopefully verifiable. Not all knowledge could be shared and tested though, as one had to prepare the mind and the soul for certain things to be understood or even perceived. Most people were afraid to look inside, the rest utterly unable. People and science hated the idea of emptiness too much, detesting that awful thought of being almost nothing but empty space... Science was emotional and arbitrary, utterly tied to and limited by the thinking of a specific time and a narrow culture. It denied subjectivity as a tool of research, and thought reality needed to only be understood, but not felt. Scientists were thus always divided! Into subject and object, mind and body, matter and energy. They never put it together, as one...Always either—or.

But since any act of observation changed the observed event itself, as quantum physics asserts, and which Tuko himself found to be true, an observer trying to make sense of the universe had to first become a *complete* observer, unlimited by specialization or established world-views. He had to become simple enough to understand the truth, which was usually quite simple also.

He was simply breathing. Looking at what was. It was all a puzzle that would come together as a whole. All the pieces had to fit, and none could be left over. Where did it all come from? Was any of it real, or was the world nothing but illusion? Projection? A hologram! Was he himself real? Well, nothing could not be aware of nothing, therefore his awareness itself had to exist—and it sure did, more than ever before! But none of this mattered; only breathing mattered. Breathing was the gateway to reality! He was breathing for many things, now...

And back he was again, deep inside himself, diving into cellular awareness, and into molecular constellations—and he stood on the surface of a world with great gravity. It had one sun that was visibly moving towards setting, and then it was dark. There were stars that moved, which had to be the electrons of atoms of the same molecular system, but there were also fixed stars. The electrons of more remote molecules. All the rest—empty, black space. And there—the sun was coming back again! He had to be on the proton surface of a hydrogen atom to experience only one sun, which just now dawned faintly on the horizon before putting in her first appearance. Amazing, how nothing much changed when the universe was looked at from inner spaces, from micro-space: Day and night, stars, sun, empty space were—much as it looked from Earth's surface, at night...Tuko sat down right there, and concentrated on breathing, looking at the quarks, meditating on the *three*, and what he found was a puzzle-piece called 'Holy Trinity'. Three was the number of creation, the creation of life! Mother, Father, Child. Three points connected, forming the second dimension—a triangle.

Tuko sat somewhere in the dark and did not know where. He focused on breathing but did not know if he was breathing oxygen or something else. Where did he belong? Was traveling the microcosm a dream, or was it all equally real, and his size the only illusion, his limitation and his arbitrary anchor? He needed to come out of the small caves now, and find the larger ones, just to get back some orientation.

Crawling out of his cave as well as out of his body proved no more difficult than going inside. It was just like coming from the atomic worlds back to the planetary one. A discrete change in size that Tuko called a *hierarchical* quantum leap, and little more difference than that. He stood on a planetary surface, earth probably, and felt himself as a part of the solar system, as all of it really. The earth was part and parcel of the solar system, spinning around the sun, as did eight other planets. A few moons behaved in just the same way—and all those bodies together gave the system its characteristic function. The sun could possibly exist without the planets, but it would not evolve its inherent qualities, such as the ability to use its energy to create the forms of life it had produced by having planets. Tuko realized that the existence of the planets was not explained by gravity or random evolution, but rather followed a script, an unseen *purpose*! And this purpose was to create life, wasn't it? There was life all over his own solar system, on planets, moons, on their surfaces, inside their hollows, and of course in their unimaginably vast realms of micro-space. This was no coincidence! He found traces of man left on some of those worlds that were older than life on earth. But the one thing that stood out as the overwhelming truth of it all, he now knew, was that the whole system itself was *alive*! It was a living thing, just as earth was a living thing—that was an undeniable, observable fact. No logic could possibly imagine living things being part of a dead machine, come to think of it. *The whole of a system will always be more complex, more intelligent, and more alive than any one of its parts! Therefore, the solar system had to be at least as complex, as intelligent, and as alive—as humans, including all of their 'inventions'.* Inevitable logic. *Why can humans not see that? How very hidden the obvious can be...Why do we not see the obvious? But then - why don't fish know water?*

With this realization, Tuko started to look around in neighboring systems, and soon realized that every single system contained ever more life and was itself alive. Life was no random fluke, but the overriding rule, the reason, the purpose and order of it all! He knew this with infinitely more certainty than he had ever felt before about anything, including basic algebra. Life was the purpose!

So, he had to ask himself—what about a galaxy, that all from its own substance and resources had produced life on even just one of its planets? Was a galaxy with so much planetary and microscopic life inside it—a dead thing? To see the Milky Way with some perspective, Tuko would have had to get *outside* of it—so he decided to stay just where he was, but knowing himself a part of that much larger, a *hierarchically* larger system. About a hundred billion stars, roughly seventy-five percent of which danced along with one or more companions, down the galactic track around an incredibly heavy center, as a great, rotating, spiraling disk. Similar again to the atomic and the solar systems; only a hierarchical difference. None of these rationalizations would ever come close to explaining how it all *felt*, of course, how the music sounded in each of the spheres, the realization of how alive it all was, and how incredible. He could feel the interconnected weave of energies that made up the Milky Way as a cave, and the glory of it was momentous with billions of participating voices. It was a comfortable cave. Huge, though...

And then he climbed out of the galaxy—not parallel to find another one of the surrounding spirals, but hierarchically *out*—to the level of galactic clusters that consisted of hundreds or thousands of galaxies! Again, he observed the rotating principle, a thousand galaxies rotating together around a center. Spin seemed to be the only way for any structure to exist in the universe... A powerful sense of aliveness ruled reality here as well, stronger even than on the smaller hierarchical levels.

And again, he crawled out of the cave that was his own galactic cluster and found a larger structure still—but it did not rotate! It had an irregular shape, and its structure was net-like, the empty space isolated in holes, or caves—and the smell of life here was overpowering. Tuko felt that this was as close as he would get to the end of it all, to the largest thing—which had to be the whole universe. Probably, nothing much would change, as long as he looked outward, from inside this universe. To see what the universe itself in fact *was*, he would have to leave it and look at it from the *outside*...He did not feel ready to do that. Nothing, by definition, was supposed to exist outside the universe. He was quite certain there had to be an *outside*, but he simply was not ready yet to leave the universe. He needed to take a piss.

Tuko opened his eyes—and saw everything near bright as day! Surely, it wasn't morning yet, it couldn't be. In fact, the entrance of the cave was bathed in darkness, while the inside alone was lit, without however hinting at a source of the light, and without casting shadows. Tuko stepped deeper into the cave that seemed to continue into the bowels of the earth, until he found a good spot to empty his bladder. No longer did he feel like an intruder, but rather like having lived here for hundreds of years, like being home. When he returned to his previous position, he heartily drank from the water-bottle, stretched his limbs a little, then closed his eyes and watched his body breathe itself.

Orientation

The vastness of the universe was too much to bear. Tuko needed to get some orientation, some understanding, some clarity on why it was all as it was, where it all came from, how it all worked. Something he could walk away with and share with others. Share with scientists. Thinking about it would not help much, however. Thought was too linear, its logic too limited—he had to use pure *seeing*, and then later try to make sense of what he had seen. He needed to breathe...

God was in the details, but the recognition of God and of the universe was in relating those details to Oneness! Science lived in a bubble of either/or, where analysis fractured reality into disconnected pieces that were all unrelated and could not be put back together again. Humans were the masters of a divided world and of isolated perspectives that made a simple view on *all* of reality quite impossible. A world full of 'specialists' that concentrated only on differences, but rarely saw the common denominators, or the simplicity of what really *was*...

How then was space created in his own experience? By climbing in and out of celestial caves, by walking to take a leak, by turning around and coming back...

And, all of a sudden, it all became clear as glass: There was something very wrong with how the world saw the 'dimensions' of space, and in his clarity Tuko realized just what was so wrong: Mathematics was limited and even distorted by ignoring the entire human experience! It all started when the scientist used only his left frontal cortex, the rational part of himself—ignoring the intuitive perceptions of the right frontal cortex and the rest of his brain and body. You needed both left *and* right to see reality for what it really was! You needed left and right just to look straight, and front and back to know your direction!

It was like walking! Walking *created* the dimensions by creating space! One step forward created the number one, the next step created the two and so on. The first dimension (length), was at the same time the creation of natural numbers, but it had two directions—*Forward* and *Backward*—defined by adding or subtracting numbers. When a human walked along like this, creating the first dimension, he of course sooner or later came to a crossroad or an obstacle. Tuko visualized a fork in the road and a sign saying Left—Right. He stood for a moment, trying to decide which way to turn, when he remembered something by an old English philosopher who had said that "when you come to a fork in the road—take it!" Did that not cut nicely through the entire illusion of either/or? Did this not deflate the suggestion that choice must be divided? Tuko looked at the sign, at the roads, the landscape between the roads, at the sky. All the solutions lay before and all around him: He could go left, and right, and straight through the treed valley ahead. He could meander along a little stream and jump across it in zigzags like a kangaroo. He could also turn around and walk back. And he could sit down by the sign and do nothing but be part of the landscape. There were a lot more options yet, and the freedom, the circumspection of it, allowed for undivided choice! It was like choosing a blueberry from a basket full of various berries, none of which would go to waste. He chose a goat-path that was barely visible along a wooded ridge skirting the valley.

This was Tuko's first lesson in space-walking. But soon the path ended at a massive rock wall that could not be climbed. Now, provided he insisted on his direction, he could only follow the path to the left around the obstacle—or go right. He stopped, and contemplated how there *always* was an end, an obstacle to any one direction in life and in nature. It was a given that at some stage, one had to face the duality of *Left* and *Right*! It was how the brain itself was structured. Left and right was called 'width' in geometry, but to see through the very nature of left/right, one had to understand how its duality related to Oneness. To humans it was always left *or* right! They wanted to be 'right' all the time, and never 'left' out; their very mind-scape was shaped by this absolute division, where politicians from the left and those of the right were irreconcilable in their views, and where the English drove on the left, or wrong, side of the road. Silly—when the world needed both left and right, just to exist! How could there be anything 'left', if there were no 'right?' Silly! The simplest truth of all this was that Left/Right was the second dimension...

When Tuko had walked around the mountainous outcrop, the path was no longer even, but instead went up and down, up and down, leading eventually towards a massive mountain range where the only way remaining was up. Height, he thought, is simply the duality of *Up/Down*. It was a given orientation in all of life, although with flexible and reversible definitions of what exactly *was* up. But up/down was the third dimension!

The fourth dimension was not time. Time did not really exist; it was simply another way to say space. One, two, three steps create the first dimension, and incidentally what we also might call time. One, two, three seconds. Whether we call it three seconds, or three meters, or three steps—there was no objective difference. Time was mostly an illusion. The fourth dimension was *spin, clockwise and anticlockwise* spin, but not time. Spin was the way to get further in space, much like a helicopter. Vortex was the principle that structured galaxies and human energy centers, and even the quarks at the bottom of material reality were defined by their spin. Tuko felt the spin of the dancing dervishes in his chakras, and his entire body, as it sat on a mountaintop, whirled wildly as if he was about to fly up into the sky. Feeling himself go lighter with increasing spin he thought that an anti-gravity machine would have to work on this same principle, as gravity and spin were aspects of each other.

Just as the first three dimensions combined as vectors (forward, right, up) always lead to a vortex, the vortex created suction and thus led to the fifth dimension—*inside/out*! On his journeys, Tuko could go inside a cave and come out. This was the orientation science missed, the crux of understanding space. Sometimes, we cannot take steps, or turn left, or climb up, or change our spin. Sometimes, we are getting born, sometimes we need to leave our bodies, sometimes the embryonic bird cracks the egg to conquer more space. Sometimes, distances don't matter because the only thing that counts in space is whether we are inside or outside any hierarchical structure. Black holes are a fine example for how first there is spin and then they turn inside/out, disappearing from inside this universe only to reappear outside of this universe. The five dimensions could comprehensively describe the universe and hierarchical space as purposeful; it was clear as a mountain spring. The fifth dimension dealt with space as a baby does when sliding out of the birth-canal! As a sock does when being reversed. Similarly, to visit another galaxy, one had to take a five-dimensional quantum-jump *out* of the planetary plane to the galactic level, rather than having to traverse the linear, if bent, space between. The *Moebius-strip* was a bizarre reduction of this inside/out, where conventional three-dimensional space fails utterly to account for the change of geography. Tuko could see other factors that could be counted as dimensions, but most of them originated in the realms of Mind, and were therefore not, to most scientists, identifiable as physical dimensions. There were only five orientations needed to create magic. Five fingers to one hand. Magic was in the obvious!

Tuko needed another piss, fully entered his body before rising and ...without taking a step, he stood already at his proper spot in the smaller room, holding his inside-out thing. How did he get here? All thought ceased with the sensation of warm urine running through and out of him. He was mostly water and he felt like water, too! He was water. And fire! Another spark of mere intent brought him straight back to his previous spot, sitting there as if he had never moved.

Fire and water

The cave was silent. But when Tuko listened deeply he could hear the water. Deep inside, there seemed to be many places where it trickled and ran, fell and cascaded, carving its environment as it went, shaping the landscape of reality. Water was everywhere, even inside his body! It trickled through the tunnels that connected his inner caves, thickly red or white or green or clear. He was a gurgling fountain, a landscape full of streams, a pot of warming water...Water had always existed, like fire. Or had it? When earth was still a glowing fire-ball, there was obviously no water. On earth. And when the universe was young, was there also no water? Did fire really come first? And as soon as he had formulated the question, Tuko saw the answer! There was no either/or! Fire and water were not, as humans thought, antagonistic opposites at all, nor did they evolve one after the other! They needed each other! There could be no fire without water, and no water without fire, because they were not even two different things! Fire was the microcosm of water! What humans saw as a droplet of water, the *observer inside the droplet* sees as a fiery sky full of sun-like electrons, and certainly nothing like a liquid. So, water as observed from *inside*, was only fire and empty space. Similarly, our sun-filled macro-universe could well be macro-cosmic water, if observed from *outside* the universe! And if no microcosm can exist without a macro-identity...and Tuko was quite sure that the principle was universal...then fire and water were two aspects of the same thing.

Water was not the antagonist of fire, but its mother. Fire, Tuko realized now, could spread on its own, but was always born of water. The heat of compost arises from its humidity. The heat of digestion required a liquid environment. Lightning—was produced by clouds full of nothing but water! The stars were burning hydrogen! And yes, fire was simultaneously created with water, since it makes up all the inner, microcosmic structure of water. Was there a fireball before any water? No, there must have been water on a higher level that could explain the fire that without water could never have existed...Why would the micro-observer inside a droplet of water ever suspect the existence of water when he sees nothing but flying electrons?

Tuko did not think he could explain this to a scientist who had not himself felt and experienced reality as he did now. Real understanding required subjective involvement and a sense for the relativity of hierarchical space that came with non-attachment to body-size, culture, time and ego. Humans were far too divided to see all the connections. He understood that he had already seen more than the science of his time with its denial of subjectivity and of most relevant cognitive pathways was even aware of. Science was too divided into irreconcilable opposites. Physics without biology made no sense. Nor did biology without physics. Medicine without psychology. All these divisions blinded one from seeing what actually *was*! God, while without doubt in the details, was still sitting far outside of creation, and the universe was still a never-ending Big Bang without any purpose. Tuko knew better, now, but he was still hunting for the larger picture by taking a fresh look at the relevant detail. What he really wanted to know was how the universe was made, and why. But there was a ceiling he could not yet get beyond. He concentrated again on his breathing and let himself go empty.

Complexity and simplicity

With the breathing slowing down, it became possible to look at this ceiling and at why he could not go further. He was not yet free enough of self-constructed limitations, still bound by the past, by imperfect attitudes that clouded perfect clarity. Not free enough to see the blue sky behind the clouds that still held his attention. He still needed to look at the clouds, and as he followed one dark cloud that suddenly passed far above, breathing very slowly now—he whirled around for a moment, and then found himself lying strapped in his cot, unable to turn onto his side. *His mother slept. He wanted to be close to his mother. Smell her. She smelled incredible. She would not come, though. And she did not like noise; crying only made her angry. He remembered climbing out of the cot before. Without falling! He was so proud. And he had crawled to and into his mother's bed, very quietly, and she was warm and smelled like everything was forever good. Then she had woken up, grown annoyed, and put him back into his cot. Now, they strapped him in, so he had to lie on his back, and he knew his mother did not want him. He was only a little over a year old, but knowing that crying was not an option, he started to study the leather-straps that held him in position. It was dark and he could not see, but his hands could, and after a while he began to figure it all out, eventually opening the two fastenings. He wriggled out of his bindings, climbed over the side of the cot and crawled to his mother's bed. This time, he made no sound, no indent in her bed, and he stopped breathing for a while, because it made his chest drum too loudly...But his mother had awoken again, put him back, and the next day she fixed the bonds so that he could not figure them out for a long time. He felt the pain in his solar plexus, that was a combination of being forced onto his back—and of knowing himself unwanted.*

Tuko came back with a deep, releasing breath. He still felt the pain in the stomach area, but noticed how breathing deeply into it, made it go away. He had never been able to sleep on his back, in all his life! Lying on his back for long had brought back the pain every time. Even the soul-pain he had carried responded to his breathing right into it. But then he became momentarily dizzy and—*he was back in his cot. But this time was before the bad stuff had all happened, still in his father's house. He was not older than six months. He was alone in his room every night. His mother was in his father's room at the far side of the house. He was wet and cold, and he cried as loudly as he could. It was like this every night. His mother never came. The problem was that a night lasted so very long when he was wet and bitterly cold! It was impossible to sleep when wet and cold, and every moment lasted an eternity. He felt he had spent lifetimes wailing at the world, feeling only hopelessness and despair. His mother never came until the next morning. The loneliness of it, the un-cried-for loneliness...*

He came back to the present, sobbing, remembering it all. He could have drawn the ground-plans for the house he had last seen at age two. And he now had an inkling of just how long an eternity felt. He remembered, and went back to breathing, in sobs first, and quietly later. He finished off his water and went deeper into the cave where he found a spot where a steady trickle made it easy to refill his bottle. He drank directly from the rock and was about to return to his spot of comfort, when he spotted a further opening that seemed to lead deeper down into the earth. He could see quite well, despite the absolute darkness, but when he hesitantly stepped into the unknown he could see nothing, not even the ground before him. The Unknown had never looked more impressive. He wanted to go back, but then he stepped into the dark and began to see a chamber about as big as his own, but far more comfortable looking and inhabited by a little lizard that suddenly darted along a wall. Tuko felt a pang of heart-warming familiarity at meeting another life-form and settled down to stay for a while. The lizard came down to the ground in a blink and now stood there, just two meters away, looking increasingly like a prehistoric dragon. He was a thing of absolute perfection, scintillating with blues and greens, and eyes big with wonder at this strange visitor. The lack of size references, as well as the intense focus of attention made the reptile suddenly appear super-sized, as if it almost filled the cave! Was he hallucinating? While a part of him knew the animal was only small, another part of Tuko simply wanted to be free of limiting conventional, conditioned, and relative perspectives, and did therefore not resist seeing a full-sized dinosaur squatting right in front of him, blinking one huge eye as if to assure him of his realness. He stared at the giant reptile, feeling his own reptilian brain awaken and relate to this messenger of a remote past. It was all somehow familiar—as if he had walked with dinosaurs before, been threatened by them, learned to live with them. Or else, he had himself been a reptilian at some stage of evolution, and now remembered himself, his own reality, as it once was. In either case, he had dinosaur-memories in his DNA that allowed him to relate to the reptilian state of mind... At this point, the lizard scuttled right up to him and climbed up his leg. He spontaneously and without reason felt overwhelmed with emotions for the little spirit, and a sense of companionship flowered when the baby-dragon climbed into his hand and trustingly rested there as if he had found a home. After a while he wriggled himself free, climbed down Tuko's leg and darted back to its favorite wall, disappearing completely into it. *Not so lifeless down here*, he reflected, still staring. So far, no bats, but Tuko scanned the ceiling anyway, occasionally... He felt more grounded now than before, and less encumbered. He smelled the bowels of the earth, the ancient past; his mind was at rest. He was an old thing. A thing from the ancient past. A thing about to completely wake up into the present.

It was so simple really, to understand how the universe was made! Simplicity itself! He could see it now. First there was One. One atom, one cell, one anything. The One divided and became two, then four and eight and sixteen. Only One was needed to create sixteen. One Word, one Sound, one thing. The rest of complexity followed. All of mathematics followed, was inherent in the One. Two created direction, three created the triangle and area and a new Oneness. Four created the tetrahedron, the pyramid, as well as the rectangle and the golden ratio of 0.618. Eight bodies, trying to be as close to each other as possible, would always create a dice, and twelve bodies created a dodecahedron. And this was all that was needed for complexity, infinite complexity! Mathematics had developed via all those platonic bodies into what it was today. But it was all implicit in the One and in the fact that all parts remembered the One and strove to become One again. Gravitation was just this desire of one body to move as closely as possible to another body! Four bodies would thus arrange themselves into a triangle, plus number four resting on top. Their connected centers then formed a pyramid. Very many cells arranged in this way eventually made up entire organisms... No God or further agency was needed! Complexity was inherent and implicit in perfect simplicity. It was all so simple, once the stone was rolling—the universe developed inevitably all by itself, without any creator or outside agency, and all it needed to do was to divide while staying One.

"Do *you* know what got the stone rolling in the first place?" Tuko asked the little dragon somewhere in the opposite wall aloud, without much hope for any answer. Indeed, he received no answer, except from the cave itself, that amplified the question and left a big silence hanging once her growl had quite subsided. A little humbled and embarrassed, Tuko quietly apologized to the cave for his...lack of respect. The cave did not like casual noise.

This and that

Breathing deeply, Tuko noticed that he was no longer cold, and since there were no mosquitoes now either, he took off his shirt, as well as the pants, and he felt warm and good. The mushrooms were coming in huge waves now. Breathing deeply, he again committed to his meditations. In and out. Yang and Yin. Everything in pairs of two: man and woman; left and right; proton and electron; life and death; man or mouse. The two creates the three, as man and woman create a baby, or simply as two steps lead up to the third. All things are made of three. Quarks, Holy Trinity, Celtic sun-cult—those were just words for all things being three. And these three made up the 'ten-thousand things' of Lao-Tzu—the universe! One needed to understand the three to understand the two, and one needed to master the two so one could get beyond duality and perceive the One! Like counting backwards. One needed to see the baby to fathom how the two parents had once been One.

With left and right it was even more obvious—there *was* no left without a right! They were *always* one. Like life and death—always one! Living things were dying constantly. The cells of the body were dying from birth, but all the dead cells, as well as all the energy went on to participate in new life. One! Two ways of looking at One; not two things...

Why did humans come as a duality, as man and woman—if not to become One; if the lesson of unification were not our ultimate purpose, our ultimate identity? Sex made One out of two, on several levels—and thus created life...maybe this was how it always was? Maybe humans were *supposed* to learn how to become One on every level? Why else would there be black, brown and white humans, if becoming One was not the deeper purpose of nature? Duality was not about any *either/or*—it was about *as-well-as*, as Tuko could now clearly see.

People saw reality as an either/or. Live, or die. But it was always both, simultaneously, wasn't it? He was already dead, he was a dying thing, and he had died before as he was dying now. Oneness...

Oneness. The universe was One, despite its complexity, and it must have been One just before it came into being and started to expand. Just before the 'Big Bang'. But was the Big Bang the original first step, the beginning of everything, the beginning of time, space and existence? This was where the physicists struggled, trying to determine that point zero where everything began from nothing. Tuko remembered vaguely all those theories he had heard about at uni, theories that presumed nothing to have existed before this universe was born. Inflation theory—a universe inflating itself from an unexplained bubble. Creation from nothing—a supernatural concept that avoided the origin problem completely. Vacuum theory—another philosophical concept of nothingness. String theory—yes that made some sense, as it pointed at the duality of strings as the mechanics of Oneness. But it was an inconclusive mathematical concept with no real connection to experienced reality, and it did not explain a thing. Steady State theory—that was more like actual reality; a universe that was not created by an explosion, but kept being created by new atoms that sprang continuously into existence. Yes, that was more like it! The universe was no explosion; it only looked like one when one observed it from inside the universe, and if one did not know what had existed before that event. The speed of an 'explosion' would actually be quite slow if the universe was seen from outside itself by a large observer...

Oneness. The universe could only be a One-thing if it was bounded. An unbounded universe could not suddenly begin to exist, as it existed everywhere and in eternity, and could then not suddenly pop from one place into another. It was in fact unlimited but bounded, just as the earth's surface provided unlimited distances despite being bounded to a definite size. Was the universe rounded or hyperbolic? Well, from the inside it may appear as hyperbolic to mathematicians, but contemplated from outside the universe certainly was round. But what *was* this thing humans called the 'universe' in reality? Definitely not a random explosion; definitely not any mystical inflation or any sudden appearance from nothing, Tuko was sure of that. But how could he understand its actual nature, its significance to humans from physical concepts? It was not all intellectual after all—to understand the universe mentally had to be just a small part of true understanding. All things came in dualities, and thus had to be not only understood but also felt! He was quite clear on this—there was an emotional part to understanding reality! Otherwise what would be the point of emotions existing inside the universe? This is what science could not perceive from within reason alone...But could *he*? Could he perceive what was not conceivable intellectually? Could he let go of his intellect for just a little while, he pondered while concentrating on breathing out all thought?

He was seven years old. A farmer had called and reported a young deer he had injured when mowing. His mother had spoken of how to bottle-feed little deer that had leg injuries, and his step-father had taken him to where it had been found. It had two legs mowed right off, but little Tuko did not see that and sat there lost in the deer's deep brown eyes, dreaming of feeding and raising the beautiful creature. When his unaware father wordlessly slid out his hunting knife to end the suffering, he did not notice. He stared into those brown eyes when the knife slid into the neck of the animal. He was very much emotionally aware of seeing those eyes break in surprised death, giving up all of their light. A universe had ended right there! He knew he could not cry or even show any sadness—or he would never be respected as a hunter, never be taken hunting again. He would be laughed at. He had gone cold inside. Later, he had never felt this way again when he hunted and killed animals...And he had never cried since that day...

Tuko's breathing had become ragged. He was becoming fully aware of how he had so long ago lost much of his emotional perception, his empathy, half his view on reality, and he breathed deeply now while holding the pain of it in his heart, only gradually releasing it after all those years...and while he was breathing and repairing himself, a new universe was gradually born! A twoness came together and revealed an entirely new Oneness, a fundamentally new universe, one that he could not only *see* but increasingly *feel*! And he realized that mistake scientists made when trying to perceive the ultimate truth: they believed the universe only had to be intellectually *understood*. But the truth was it had to be *felt* also! Was it not so with all micro-universes—like for instance a woman? To try and 'understand' her, to analyze her composite parts, and to speculate where she came from—did not really give a man the slightest clue on who she *was*. Only by means of deep emotional connection, by the Oneness of spirit, by feeling her profoundly—could anybody learn to perceive the essential truth of that particular universe which was that woman. Tuko was not thinking now, he just *saw*. He saw how all the dualities came together. Just as the universe had to be understood and felt, the observer also had to be objective *and* subjective. A scientific error of this era...They were of course quite correct about objectivity, where theories needed to be verified and widely agreed on. But first, the observer had to be utterly aware of his subjectivity, and to get there he needed to get fully involved with his object of observation to the point where he could feel it's inner truth and become one with it! Only through interacting and feeling anything came true understanding, true inside perception. Objectivity at this point could only lead to division between subject and object, and thus prevent the cognitive process. Only after diving personally into the depth of what could be subjectively perceived should any scientist begin to show and verify to others objectively what he has found! Objectivity followed subjective experience. True science required a scientist with the courage to let go, to perceive beyond the mental cultural views he was programmed to. A scientist who could experience reality with all the intact senses of a child, a scientist who had no illusions about himself and therefore really knew how to subtract his subjectivity when the time came for sharing and objective verification. Science in his time divided but forgot to put back together again. It was big with analysis, but short of unification, of comprehension, unable to see the whole picture for the masses of over-identified particles...

Tuko knew that at this very moment he was the ultimate observer on earth. He did not think it, he just knew while he was breathing and feeling. He became more and more aware that it would never do for an observer to look in an incomplete or prejudicially limited way when trying to perceive the complete, universal, final truth. Microscopes and technology generally were far too peculiar and narrow in their presumptions; they changed what was there to see. Similarly, the scientist himself looked in peculiar, idiosyncratic ways that only reflected his subjective views but not what was actually out there. A greedy or impatient scientist would thus jump to early conclusions, the anxious scientist did not dare to be passionately involved and stayed separate, and the prejudiced scientist would find exactly what he always wanted to find, but never the opposite thereof. A materialistic scientist would not become aware of qualitative reality and an idealistic one would impose his ideals on what actually *was*. Tuko realized with a pang that he was not at all prepared. There were still thoughts that would catch his breath, and form tiny obstacles to free and delightful flow of thought and perception. He was still too conditioned! Sure, he had thrown out most of his own culture's prejudices by traveling, had outgrown his early childhood programs fed to him by Catholic parents and society, and he had spent much time in nature and with animals, which had cleared him of the usual human arrogance that arose in self-important isolation of race or species. But he still had prejudices, conditioned views that clouded further insights. He saw reality from a male point of view, for instance, which trapped him into one of the most powerful dualities of all! The universe could not be comprehended by such division, by an observer who saw only with half a soul...

There were other prejudices, too, and kinks in attitude, shortcomings and divisions. But no matter how long the list of weaknesses was—this list would not continue to exist into the future! There was only the *now*, and any thought of deference or postponement simply did not occur because it did not belong here. As soon as Tuko now became aware of a hitch in his breath over any arising image, he tried to completely face the lesson that he felt was coming up and needed to be learned. By facing the discomfort while breathing deeply, a chemical change happened every time deep inside himself, like a knot opening. Eventually, every bad, wrong or weak feeling gradually disappeared, until almost only clarity remained.

Boys and girls

As a red-blooded Austrian male, Tuko had a particularly hard ride facing the strict division of humans into gender that so determined perspective. He identified with being male. He loved women, but found many of them silly, clingy or vague, and apart from sex he often preferred the company of male friends. Only in some tantric experiences had he seen a glimpse of that Oneness that allowed him to really feel the woman he was with, but it wasn't enough. He was so much more yang than he was yin, and he needed to attain that perfect balance. He asked the question and focused on his breathing, understanding by now that every question inevitably created its corresponding answer, just as the answers formulated all the questions. He was creating himself new, repairing all the cracks, just by breathing. He had the magic wand, he was guided, just by breathing. In and out, in and out, ever so slowly, he proceeded on his path to end all division.

Suddenly, he was in a great, high-ceiling chamber in what seemed like a five-hundred-year-old French or Bavarian castle. He was brushing his long, blond hair as he walked toward a large gold-framed mirror. As he looked up, he saw a beautiful woman in a long, elegant sleeping gown, holding a hair-brush, astonishment painted over her face. He instantly fell very deeply into this new reality, temporary amnesia suspending his previous identification with being a man. He had memories, so new, so very strange. Memories of being a woman. A duchess of all things! Memories of having sex with her lover, of all the sensations involved. She continued brushing her hair, lost in her precious memories. Absently, she patted the heads of both hunting dogs that had trotted up to her from the open fire. She touched her breast, adjusted it, did a half-turn to check on the firm roundness of her behind and wondered what she had forgotten...oh, yes!

Tuko was back in a leap, touching his chest, then his balls, breathing heavily. When he got up and went to drink from the wall, he could still feel his hips moving in strange ways, his upper body held back unnecessarily. He thought good God what next, but was acutely aware of how his view on reality was still changing fast. Had he been a woman in a previous life? All those memories, those sensations—they had to come from somewhere, they were too consistently detailed to be only imagined. And still now—he could perfectly feel the world from a woman's perspective! Why did that surprise him so, he wondered. Of course, he had to have lived many lives before this one! Nobody just popped out of the woodwork an original worm. Nothing and nobody was created from a vacuum, originally created from nothing. Even the laws of known physics ascertained that energy could not be created or lost, only changed. Humans too did not begin to exist with the birth of their bodies—they were eternal! Humans had always existed, from all beginning. Before the first microorganism! Naturally, nobody kept being reborn as one and the same gender or species over and over. One had to walk through it all...And he had likely lived as often as a woman as he had as a man!

And even now, he realized, he was not entirely a male. He had male and female hormones like every other human; he was once a female as an embryo, and he had nipples therefore. When he had had tantric sex—he had *felt* what it was like to be a woman, as he had felt it when he had still been inside his mother. Men just had a tad more testosterone and a tad more dangle; otherwise they were not that different, were they? The actual difference was rather minute, he thought with his female brain and giggled a little. Why did people identify so exclusively with one gender to the point of being blind for Venus when they're on Mars? Ridiculous! Blinding! The curse of division. Unmastered duality! He wiped the delusion of gender division right off his to-do list, knowing he would never fall for it again. Humans were always both male *and* female, and so was he. Another duality becoming One. He was getting closer...

It was in this confident moment, that Tuko felt a strong, scaly body slowly slither by his right foot, touching just enough for him to know this was no lizard. The snake had found him! He quickly looked at his old feelings of defensive fear, that hung there like old memories waiting to be fed with actual emotion. He smiled at his old memories, at what he had thought survival instincts. There was no enemy, no threat, no reason to be defensive! This was not the scary snake of his previous life that would have threatened him enough for him to react and jump and roll his eyes; no, this was the snake that belonged here and that had decided to check out this new occupant of her cave. It was most likely a cobra, but he could not quite see, it was now more dark than it was not. She was calm, curious, trusting and gentle, Tuko thought. Her touch not being resisted, it felt to him like waves of snake-ness seeping into his leg, conveying what it was like to be a snake. Her body did not seem to end when it slid slowly past his ankles, generously giving him of herself—and then, suddenly, she was gone. He had been *touched*, and it was profoundly good. There was really no cause for alarm. The snake was not an enemy, not a threat at all. She was life! He smiled.

When Tuko next went to the drinking wall, he learned to *see* with his feet. It would not do to step on anything alive, he thought. It began with his feet knowing just an instant before they touched the ground what they would touch. Or rather—he would remember his future awareness of what he *had* touched... It was strange, but he then just accepted the fact itself, as it helped him to walk around quite naturally, even without the bright light of consciousness always on. It was an animal instinct coming to life. He realized that it would not do to see reality only from a human perspective or walk around like a bumbling human. One had to travel through the minds of animals and become acquainted with their skills and their senses in order to more completely understand reality. The truthfulness and loyalty of dogs, the social and cultural abilities of ants, the non-aggressive surrender of snakes—it was all part of what he had to learn, part of the complete picture he could obtain from the universe. It was a suddenly obvious insight. He was walking, now, as if he meant it.

One or the other

There was absolutely no point thinking about any of it. Thinking only regurgitated old information and mixed it all up in a wild pattern of personal projections. He sat down where he was, breathing. Aware of his humanness, his animal self, and of the weaving in between that made them both one and the same in principle. An intensely earthy, slightly acidic taste in his mouth carried him on a wave of blissful surrender to an oblivion of recent data and an extermination of all separate self-recognition. To be stuck in time or even in one's own species was to be prejudiced and confined. He could not be this or that and he breathed deeply through the pain of not being what he needed to be.

He first felt his skull-plates move slightly against each other, down along the center of his skull, instantly causing a considerable alteration in awareness. Then his skull seemed to change shape, flattening at the forehead, and thickening. His jawbones similarly began to grow more powerful, much as he weirdly remembered this from werewolf movies, and a new strength filled his body, a new awareness. He was an ape, or a Neanderthal, a hairy being, a wild thing, a thing so strong its strength threatened to carry him with it. He was hungry! Hungry and hairy, and near ready to run where there was delicious food and blood-heating company...

But there was, deep down, an important memory of the past, ever so vague, or was it the future, that was more than this, that was more than real, or was it not? More real than eating or rooting? Yes, yes there was something... Breathing! That was it, yes! Tuko let himself slide to the cave-floor, curling up like an embryo, going with the feeling of emptying and filling himself. All worldly orientation disappeared completely now, and there was only *in* and *out*, expansion and contraction.

He was now an organism of only one cell, expanding, contracting, breathing, being alive and conscious of only that fact. Nothing else mattered. Simultaneously, he was an old man, dying, taking his last few shuddering breaths, never knowing there would be another... Life streaming in, life streaming out... Everything of any importance was somehow like that – in and out, life and death, beginning and end. Out – letting go of life, of control, of individuality. In – filling up with life, being it all at once. Always reversing the inside and the outside, the landmarks of reality.

And then, still an old man dying, the fatal, final contractions became too strong, too overwhelmingly strong. The entire universe was pulsing and pushing him, an earthquake that threatened to take it all away, threatened to divide and destroy everything that was whole and good. Now, he was really dying! He felt exquisitely helpless, scared beyond cognition, and thrown beyond all reference of time. The contractions were now all that there was, and the certainty of impending death made every quivering wave of it seem the very last. Everything had been so good, so acceptable up to now, but this was to be the end of it all, the end of things being good and right and warm and stable. Things were inexorably nudging him on and on, forcing the inevitable event of the Unknown, and taking him further and further and further away from what had once been whole and safe. It was indeed all over! Death! There were powerful monsters in the dark, attacking, biting, chasing him. Intent to finish him off by squashing him, suffocating him. Part of him wanted to hurry back to find this lost place of goodness again, but another part had already lost faith with that wholeness that could be broken and just wanted to escape those monsters by running wherever they were pushing him.

At the same time, he felt the contractions in his belly, painful and terrible, but inside not outside. Still death though, immediate and final. He had to let it go or – die here and now! There was no later, no earlier, no conditions and no solace. Only struggle and surrender, only pain or surrender. Then, there was only surrender! Surrender of all fear and pain, surrender of life itself. He was giving birth to all he never was, to all the hidden parts of himself!

Then there was the brightest light he'd ever seen! Or was it all he remembered ever seeing? He was *two* now, no longer *one*. There was a very different kind of loud noise and it was very not-warm. He had been holding his breath for an incredibly long time, it seemed, but now, after everything was gone, after all life had been expelled, a huge pressure reminded him of his inside, of the vacuum there that needed to be filled. It rushed in like a torrent along with his first breath, a torrent that spoke life to all the dead of eternity and filled everything up in its wake. He was *alive*. Alive! But he was *two* and he was alone, completely alone. He cried because he felt so very alone, cried for the lost goodness, the warmth, the perfection of being *one*. He was looking through closed eyes, grasping with useless fingers for the *One* he had lost and could no longer find a trace of. He was alone and totally helpless. Alone and crying with the sadness of it. And then, when there was almost no hope at all left in him – he was lifted into this strange universe, and his face came to rest on something warm and sweet, that smelled like ultimate salvation, like hope and trust and safety, like all he had lost came back to look for him. He grasped for it with all he had, including his mouth, his arms and hands, and suddenly all was good again. The goodness was back! Two can be One, he thought in the simple version of a newly born... The heavenly elixir ran down into him and he moaned gratefully with relief and new hope. He was indeed alive and no longer alone.

Truth and illusion

Something had died inside him. Maybe it was something in the pattern of dripping water in the distance that softly whispered of it. Tuko did not understand at first what it was. Maybe it was his fear of death that had died, or the illusions of what he had thought important or even relevant. Something had gone still, and something else had come alive. And the world had changed beyond recognition! He could really *see* now how it was all about oneness and twoness, and about life and truth. He also saw the thousands of illusions he had maintained for all his life cracked wide open, revealing the growing kernel of the true fruit. Behind that lifting curtain of departing human illusions now lay the great truth spread out like a landscape. Seeing the truth was a view that enticed to be walked, not just beheld, but right now to just look , to just be, was far more than enough!

Once, he had thought of truth as utterly subjective and relative. A projection of the observer's own mind. There had been no absolute or objective truths anywhere. Only 'opinions', which were really ego-based projections. Now, he saw just how hard the great truths were trying to reveal themselves! If only the divided ego did not much prefer the illusions...democracy for instance—the rule of the masses! The rule of a deluded, brainwashed, selfish and immature majority! The illusion that the majority knows what they are doing! Or 'freedom', where there are only masters and slaves and fake news and corrupt secrets and prisons for those who had no privilege. One of the great truths was that humans had become masters of a divided world and were quite clueless about how to make it One again...The root of all 'evil' was division—us and the 'others'! This alone created all the wars. And on an individual level, humans fought between the sexes, between the ages, between the religions, the political borders, between the opposites of everything and every position in existence. And only because they could not perceive Oneness, only division...

The truth was a dying value...Opinions and titles owned false 'truths' that so readily became public or scientific opinion. Spin had long replaced the seeking of truth and the media presented such fake and narrow truths that it reflected nothing but the cultural, religious and patriotic agendas of those in power. In schools, truth-seeking was replaced by utterly uncritical swallowing of second-hand 'knowledge', and the senses were reduced to only a trace of what other animals had available to them. Truth was that humans got everything as wrong as could only be imagined. Especially in education, where most of a child's potential went unrealized and unnoticed, and in medicine, where mind and body were so strictly separated that medicine with its mechanistic view of the body as a machine failed to realize that thoughts and emotions were what ruled the health of the body, that every hormone was in fact an emotion. Tuko now realized just how completely illusory everything was that people believed, that he had once believed. Most of all those personal things people take so very seriously, like somebody hurting their ego, or 'making' them angry or jealous. Self-importance! That was the number one divider! To take oneself important was to be blind to any truth beyond one's own wishful and fearful thinking. So many truths were hidden behind those illusions—a fear behind every anger; a weakness behind every aggression; an uncertainty behind every confident belief...There was again this duality! A relativity between truth and illusion, where every dropping of the illusion freed up one's view upon the blue sky of ever greater truth. *Another great truth was that the opposite of any truth must also be true!* The sun rises in the morning. It also sets in the evening. Or—in order to reach higher up, one has to first bend the knees, then jump... The last will be the first... What has a beginning must also have an end. What expands, must also contract! Like, for example, the universe...

Bohr said once, Tuko remembered, that the opposite of a great truth must also be true. Amazing, he thought, that nobody realized what this actually meant! And that it applied not only to 'great' truths but to all truth! A truth was only true when its opposite was also true. *That* was relevant! The concept of a 'good' god necessitated the concept of a devil as much as there had to be a proton for every electron, a quark for every anti-quark, a micro-space in every macro-space. An up for every down. But was there really an opposite to *all* things? Clearly, to see the truth was to be equally aware of both opposites, rather than deciding for only one side. Seeing and identifying with only one side of the truth meant war, illusion, and blindness. The essential truth in life was all about rejecting the either/or view that all humans shared and to adopt an as-well-as view on reality! That was all that needed to be done to shed illusion and to reveal the great and the small truths. Tuko saw this now with the precision of a never imagined clarity, saw it as the universal solution to all medical, social, economical, psychological and philosophical problems.

But why was reality like that? Why was everything a paradox of opposites? And what came first? Fire or water? Heaven or earth? The chicken or the egg? He realized he had to drop this 'or' right out of his vocabulary. There could never be a chicken and no egg. Or an egg without the chicken that laid it! Could it! The solution was always in seeing the Oneness. The error in the chicken/egg question was the assumption of a beginning, he could see that now. He could *see* everything he looked at...

Tuko had always been committed to the truth; he didn't lie to himself. He did not mind being criticized. He looked, and then thought. He didn't jump to conclusions and he verified what could be verified. Now, his commitment to truth grew even deeper, so deep he could smell frankincense and sacred silence all around and in himself. He would test and verify later, he pledged, but for now, he would mostly just look, look where nobody may have looked before...Was really everything a duality of opposites, though? Everything? What about a tree?

And then, he had another sudden insight: There was no static duality to reality at all! Instead, all things simply *moved towards* their opposite! As the young move towards getting old, so did life move towards death, man towards woman, and so did an Easterly direction get us to the West eventually. Yin always moved towards yang. And all of the reverse. Which meant death moved towards life. Protons became electrons. Beginnings follow every end. So—what about a tree? What were its opposites and how did they move towards each other? How can any natural form, be it tree or fox or buffalo, be a duality of opposites—if what he *saw* was correct? Many mystics in history had spoken about Oneness, he recalled, and surely the sorcerers of old had also discovered that the human mind could go anywhere, see anything, and create reality at the quantum level. But none of them seemed to have answered the age-old questions satisfactorily, or even conclusively. Bits and pieces, but not the whole picture. Not in scientific terms. Why was that? Surely, they must have realized that science and magic were the same thing, that it was all about the simplest laws of the game, the laws of nature? He was not interested in this and that any more. Tuko had his intent on the law that made One out of two. The force that could make two out of One.

The quantum mechanics of Form

*All diverging opposites eventually start to approach each other, like two people walking away from each other on a globe. Opposites are thus 'mutually attractive,' always eventually reversing their identity...*Tuko looked at this like a physicist now. He wanted verifiable answers, not just personal experience! He stared hard at this paradox of how the two can be one, allowing the paradoxical to change his very brain, to make necessary adjustments in how he perceived reality. Breathing now without any interference from unwanted emotions or thoughts, he knew that simplicity was the key, that the truth was never really hidden. Again, he saw the tree and it was an apple tree. And then, all of a sudden, he knew. He knew with absolute certainty.

It was all about *form*! The form of the apple tree! The symmetries, particularly the broken symmetries of form. It was all quite simple really: Every natural form had two planes of existence. There was a minimum and a maximum to every form! There was the apple tree itself, and there was its seed that contained the precise blueprint of the mature tree! The tree, as known and perceived by humans, was only the maximum of the form *tree*, while the tree known to the seed was its minimum, a minimum that knew precisely how to move towards its maximum... *The form of every living thing expands and contracts continuously*, thought Tuko, and wondered what Plato would have thought had he realized this fundamental truth about his 'eternal forms'...Genetics explained the *eternal* nature of Plato's forms as a constant fluctuation between the minimum and the maximum of each and every natural form! The genes inside the seed were an exact copy of the maximum form of tree; there was a perfect symmetry between the genetic or microcosmic tree and the mature tree humans could see. The difference in *hierarchical size* was the *only* difference. The design itself was identical at both ends! But, at any stage during the growth of the tree from *minimum* to *maximum*, this perfect symmetry appeared broken...This was how many physicists described the universe! It had the same broken symmetries...

Tuko realized that the genes of any form are not 'dead', but as alive as their maximum. There was as much consciousness in an apple seed as there was in the mature tree, and this consciousness was what drove the will to expand, to grow into 'outer space'...To those microcosmic units carrying their design, or consciousness, towards growing into a mature tree, the expansion of their universe had to be immense and take a very, very long time.

Eventually, when the tree has matured, its form has reached its maximum. And then—the mature form contracts, implodes, and shrinks down to its minimum very fast, overnight almost! As soon as a seed forms, the maximum of the form tree has contracted itself back into the microcosm, to become its minimum again! Precisely as the Chinese see the One as consisting of the polar opposites of yin and yang...When yin grows too strong, it becomes yang. When yang grows too strong, it becomes yin. The tree, and every other living thing, were forms that derived their immortality from an oscillation between micro- and macrocosm! But why was he, Tuko, so sure that this was relevant to how the universe at large behaved? The mechanics of living forms he was seeing were surely only of biological relevance...It was just genetics, after all...

Two deep breaths cleared his mind of thinking, for just an instant. And then he saw the absolute generality of those mechanics that forms employed to stay eternal: *All* forms followed those mechanics, not just living forms! All forms had a minimum and a maximum, even man-made things like a table, a guitar or a computer, because in order to be made they had to pre-exist in the mind of the creator—which is in the microcosm of human consciousness! In order to make a table, the carpenter had to *see* the finished table (maximum) in his mind first (minimum), and know everything about it! The quality of wood, the technique of working the wood, the final varnish, all had to pre-exist, which meant that the form 'table' absolutely had to exist as a minimum before it could grow into a finished table. It was impossible for a table to come into existence without this 'seed', this blue-print on the microcosmic plane of human neurological/chemical processes. Only the *design* enables the table to grow towards its maturity, using all the environmental help it can get (like a carpenter). And then the table stands in the living room. And every visitor that sees the table–walks away carrying in his mind with him its form! Even when they have left the house, they can still see the table in their mind! The form table uses the onlooker to contract back into its minimum, so it can be carried away and—reproduced. Allowed to grow towards another maximum! And like the table, so *every* other form in the universe behaved in this same way...

Forms had been largely forgotten since Plato, as they seemed to have no permanence, no quantifiable reality. To physics, forms had seemed irrelevant. But now, this had all changed! Tuko was aware of how forms with a minimum and a maximum were an absolute game-changer for scientific thought. And he became increasingly conscious of one thing—the universe also had to have a form! And this form had to behave in much the same way as all the forms it contained.

The comprehensible universe

The form of the entire universe had to be explained by the forms it contained, just to be consistent, just to be comprehensible. All things were connected, and that excluded a completely separate reality and a separate form of the universe as compared to any of its parts. If the universe at large were not exactly as it was inside itself, it would lack connection, simplicity and comprehensibility. No, the universe was clearly a comprehensible one. A fractal one, where the parts mirrored the whole. If the universe were not comprehensible to humans, the questions about origin and purpose could not even arise. Humans could not discover truths like 'laws of nature' if the universal reality were not comprehensible. But they did! This meant that humans could 'read' from their own natural environment what the universe was all about! Their observer-horizon was representative for the larger picture! Every puzzle-piece hinted at the complete picture, which was the universe, the ultimate reality, the result of what humans called 'evolution'. The mature universe.

Was it inevitable that the universe followed the same rules of form as the apple tree and all other forms inside the same universe? How could it possibly be otherwise? Form is form, and if the universal form behaved totally differently, that would make it an incomprehensible, inconsistent universe that could never be fractal. Therefore, the form of the universe had to follow the same mechanics as all forms inside the universe. It had to grow to maturity and then contract, and grow again, and contract—like all other forms. It had to have a minimum and a maximum. The Big Bang was then the last minimum, the point where the contracted universe started to expand again as it had done countless times before, possibly forever. Symmetry plus fluctuation was form in continuity, and the broken symmetries of physics were broken temporarily only because of their at any stage incomplete movements towards their polar opposites. The opposite of the truth was always true, also, and the truth was never sterile therefore. The solution to nearly all cosmological riddles lay in the form of the universe and its mechanics! Thus, the small was determined by the vast and vice versa, which described a reality quite different from the linear evolution of cause/effect mechanics from an absolute point zero that science believed in. The fundamental human error was in the assumption of a point zero where nothing existed before this point. This was blatantly wrong. Universal realities had existed much longer than the latest expansion of *this* universe suggested.

Unification of the four forces

There were only two fundamental forces: Expansion and contraction. The four forces of physics were really only two. Tuko, breathing steadily, realized that he was not mentally formulating anything more than what the ancient Chinese did long ago with their symbol of equal opposites—yin and yang. He needed to look closer if he was to ever verify what might so easily become a purely mystical personal revelation that could never be verified! Half the work on such 'Unification' had already been done by Alan Guth and others, who were able to correlate the weak nuclear force with electromagnetism. What remained was to relate the strong nuclear force with gravitation... Nobody had so far succeeded in finding the connection, the correlation that would explain so much, and would finally allow physics to recognize the four forces as phenomena resulting from only two basic forces—expansion and contraction.

As soon as Tuko had formulated the question correctly, supremely aware of his even breath, it became clear to him how gravity was related to the strong force: While a universe expanded, its gravitational potential grew and grew, until the universe reached its maximum size. The gravitational potential at this point determined the potential explosive force scientists called the 'Big Bang' of the next universe simply by collapsing, by contracting all this gravitational potential down to the minimum in microcosmic space where it held together the nuclear fabric of that new space. The growing yang of expansion was at all stages accompanied by a contracting yin into micro-space. He could see how the gravitational potential of the expanding universe of today was responsible for the strong force of *this* universe, but how could this be mathematically demonstrated? Tuko wanted his insight to be share-able, to be objective. He took another slow breath and focused on how the size of the expanded universe related to the size of its smallest (original) building-block just as the strong force related to gravity. The radius of the universe, he remembered, was calculated from the age of the universe, which was about 13 billion years of expansion, at the speed of light (1.3×10^{10}). One light-year was 9.4×10^{12} km. The radius of its smallest building-block—the atomic nucleus(Tp)—was calculated at 10^{-13}. Dividing the radius of the universe by the radius of the nucleon should, if he saw this correctly, produce the same ratio as given by the strong force in relation to gravitation: $\underline{10^{41}}$

Tuko used a cave wall as his blackboard and visualized the numbers in shining white.

Radius of the universe / Radius of the nucleon =

$=12.22 \times 10^{22} \times 10^{5}$ cm divided by 10^{-13} cm

$= 1.22 \times 10^{28} / 10^{-13}$

$= 1.22 \times \underline{10^{41}}$

Wow! Tuko stared at the figures and went through it all again—with the same result. So—It could actually be proven, or at least demonstrated mathematically that the forces of physics were an inevitable consequence of the 'mechanics of form' as he called it for himself. Form expanded and contracted and these two forces alone were responsible for all other forces of physics. Wow!

What this meant to science was mind-blowing to say the least! Tuko wished he was a better mathematician though; in his current state of clarity he would surely find any algorithm that scientists might be interested in...But he wasn't a great mathematician, he could only do his ad hoc best. There was still a question-mark left, though: It would have seemed mechanically more reasonable for the radius of the *fully expanded, previous, universe*, in proportion to its smallest part to equal the strong force of *this* universe! At this time, though, the universe was far from fully expanded. Being at any time ruled by a possibly constant proportion of 10^{41} meant that gravitation was changing in proportion with the radius of universal expansion. Bottom line was that the strong force relative to gravitation was equal to *the radius of today's universe divided by the radius of today's nucleon*, which was the mathematical solution to Unification of all the forces of physics...He vaguely remembered that the Nobel Prize for physics had all but been guaranteed to those who could relate the strong force to gravity, but he was suddenly tired of the numbers, the mental focus of it all in the frontal cortex. Breathing was far more important... The rational part of the brain was only a hindrance to actual *seeing*, to intuition, to the purity of truth he felt deep inside the center and as a warm awareness resting against the back of his brain. He was also quite clearly using parts of his brain that had lain dormant until now and he was getting sick of using only the logical faculties ...He was *mostly* using and building those new neurological pathways now, intuiting how to construct them and using the logical frontal cortex only to translate back into share-able parameters as his loyalty for social and scientific thought suggested...

The key was simplicity! Breathing. Letting go of the mind...

The living universe

There was no time. There was only eternity, with past and future all wrapped up in one ever-changing creation event. Time was nothing but changing emotions and changing states of mind. When the mind was empty, time could not exist. *There is no sense of time left in me, only that stillness that contains everything. I have always been. I will always be. I am. My questions are all gone. I am the answer. I am breathing all the answers to long forgotten questions. I am ancient beyond comprehension and in the constant process of being born. I am the connection between heaven and earth. I am the foot the snake touches while slowly sliding along my ankle.*

When Tuko opened his eyes everything was dark. He slowly felt with his hands for the snake, gracefully lifted it up and deposited its weight on his lap. Yes, it was probably a cobra, judging by its length and weight, but he was so in tune with the creature, so intimately aware of its nature, that he never gave it a second thought. Instead, he was deeply content holding this *life* and to feel its limbless minimalist perfection, its careful intimacy and its trusting curiosity. As if the earth herself had personally reached out to him with one of her blessing fingers. Tuko caressed the snake while she explored the surfaces of his body and then very gradually slid off and left him with a sense of continued connectedness and companionship.

The earth is a living thing, and so are the stars and the galaxies. They are all there for a purpose and as parts of a larger Whole. None of them are unnecessary, each one needed. And if even only a tiny part of a galaxy is alive, then the galaxy itself is necessarily also alive, as a whole system is always at least as alive, as complex, as intelligent as any of its composite parts! And a universe that contains life cannot possibly be a dead machine, a random explosion. It is so obvious: THE UNIVERSE IS ALIVE! At least as alive as a chicken, a frog, or a human. A whole can be no less than a part of that whole... The universe has clearly created life, while explosions or inflations from nothing just don't. The universe contains life because it is itself a living thing!

Tuko caught his breath and sat up straight. There was darkness and there was light. The snake was elsewhere but the earth still reached out, penetrated him with her fragrance of certain death and impending rebirth. The cave felt pregnant with awareness, its walls almost comedic in their building expectation. The earth's fragrance was almost sweet, and it was sacred, Tuko knew with an absolute certainty beyond all reason. Wasn't it strange that he had always felt that way but had never been fully aware of it? Wasn't it strange that other people never noticed the sacredness when it arose? Disillusioned with their invented and now dying gods, they rejected everything sacred along with the religious, and those still believing in what had filled their childhood brains now knew as 'sacred' only what religious institutions wanted to sell. But still—the incense burned in Balinese temples had given Tuko a similar, if much fainter, sense of the sacred, as had the frankincense wafting through the Dom in Graz and the herbal fragrances in the high mountains of Steiermark. He drank the dripping water from the nearby ledge and that too was a sacred act. *Everything was alive! Every part of a living organism is alive.* That is why the universe had a purpose...When he went for a piss, he thought *I am water*, and so is the universe, and felt himself flowing inside/out into the world, giving all of himself away, holding nothing back. Still sacred, still beyond himself, he walked in the dark like a High Priest about to perform an ancient ritual he knew nothing about but was discovering step by step with complete faith.

The cave was a god-made cathedral, its irregular walls rococo complexities pregnant with symbolic hints that in all their nooks and crannies held answers and questions to the ultimate mysteries. Everything was alive, everywhere he looked! Even the rock itself held memories of itself, of animals, of human awareness. Memories he could *feel*. Past feelings, long gone for humans, but still alive in the present...Stones were messengers from the past, whispering silently into the ever-present future, to those few still enough to listen. Feet walking on stone always left an imprint, and always picked up imprints held by the stone...*Everything is alive*...To walk *right*, Tuko felt, was to make the stone happy, or else the spirits imprinted there...so he walked like a High Priest, like a God of Nature, deeper into his cave, with supreme trust, inhaling deeply on the incense-like fragrance that guided him.

He was deep into the cave now, deep inside the body of Earth. It was a holy act to penetrate ever deeper into what seemed like all there was, all that ever would be. He did not hit his head when the cave narrowed into a low passage. He felt the rock; there was no need to see. He felt the stalactites and he felt water dripping, and then he was in another chamber. Here, the sacred fragrance was even stronger, intimate, all-encompassing.

Everything inside the universe is alive. The universe itself is alive! It is a living organism! Life is no exception, it is the ruling principle of the universe, of reality! If the universe can be at all understood by what we can observe, it has to be a living thing, has to hold up the principle of life as paramount. A whole can never be less complex than any of its parts...There is only life! Even the rocks are not dead things; they are part of the whole body. They hold memories, they fall to dust and feed other living things. Only the illusion of time makes this difficult to perceive. How could anybody possibly believe in a dead universe that can evolve and contain such intricacies as animals and plants and human beings? In a hierarchical (box in a box) universe—a fractal universe—the Whole can be recognized by its fractal parts. I am a fractal of the universe.

Suddenly, Tuko remembered a passage from the Chinese three-five calendar where Xu Zhen wrote:

Heaven and Earth are all mixed up like an egg, and Pan Gu is born therein. After eighteen thousand years, Heaven and Earth separate. The clear yang becomes Heaven, and the murky Yin becomes Earth, and Pan Gu is in the middle, undergoing nine changes every day. The spirit is in Heaven, the sage is on Earth. Every day heaven rises by one zhang, and Earth sinks by one zhang. Thus, for eighteen thousand years, Heaven becomes exceedingly high, Earth exceedingly deep, and Pan Gu exceedingly tall. Hence, Heaven is ninety thousand li from Earth.

Was this not almost exactly true? Scientists may have found that the calculations here led to much the same result that modern physicists accepted as the age of the universe–but Pan Gu inside the egg was obviously put down to foreign or ancient superstition. Taken literally however...

If the universe had a minimum and a maximum – was not Pan Gu the human minimum that evolved towards its maximum? By asking questions like – what *is* the universe? And why would the universe be at all comprehensible to humans, if humanity were not at its minimum that remembered it all?

Tuko sat down where he stood. He was stunned! Pan Gu was humanity, and humanity was what drove the universe to expand. Humanity was the minimum of the Cosmic Human Form, and the universe itself was–a human baby! An embryo! God? In any case–the maximum! *I am not breathing!* Nothing was more important than breathing. He took a breath in three shuddering gulps, rolled onto his knees, touching the surprisingly smooth ground with his forehead, and went with his breath, which meant he was sobbing, his heart pounding far outside and around his body, breath being the only guide.

Every human is a necessary part in the DNA of God. Each one of us is necessary. 'God' is at the far end of the human spectrum, the goal of the evolution of the Human Form. God is male. He is a baby yet to be born. Tears dripping into the ancient dust, Tuko cried with the unutterable pain of complete release, unbearable joy threatening to crush everything in him that was too fragile. *I am the one who is breathing! Everything comes and goes. Let it go...*Just to *be* had become near impossible to bear. And never had he needed a friend more than in this moment! *If only I could speak to another human!* He thought about looking for the snake, but he was too far away, and the snake probably wouldn't have been so surprised at all by what to him was the complete revelation of the pen-ultimate secret to mysticism, religion, human existence, life and God.

The old shaman

I wish I could talk to a human. He sat with his eyes closed and calmed his breathing to the flow where he was most alive, when suddenly, a quiet voice spoke from nearby: "What are you doing here?" Tuko, feeling like an ant on a suddenly reversed sock, opened his eyes in disbelief and saw a sitting figure leaning against the cave wall he was facing. He was an old man with long white hair, but as Tuko watched him comfortably slouching into the rock, his face did not seem old or tired at all, with wrinkles and ancient skin tanned to a healthy, almost glowing hue of undying energy. His face reminded Tuko of his grandfather, but it also wore the expression of a tribal shaman or a holy man, a perception which was accentuated by the sparse, home-made clothes from natural materials that hung around his loins and covered his shoulders.

He is either human or ghost or spirit or a hallucination, Tuko tried to cope with this dramatically new reality. *I have created him with my wish, no matter what he is...* But this was not now a time for scientific investigation; this was an opportunity to talk to a person, whether he be alive or dead or an unconscious part of himself! And this person had asked him a question...

"I belong here", he replied with a voice he barely recognized as his own.

"So this is your cave now?" said the old shaman in a voice that might have held an edge of threat, but actually sounded warm and accepting, when Tuko thought of it.

"Yes, my cave."

'How do you think you earned the right to call this cave your own?'

"I have given all I had to the cave, and the cave accepted me by giving me all or more I could bear." Tuko did not feel like arguing ownership or personal importance. "Do you live here?" He had felt no human presence here before and was quite sure no human had been here earlier.

"I live everywhere. I live here, I'm dead here, and alive here; I exist and I do not exist", the old man whispered with an almost-smile ghosting through wrinkles that seemed to elaborate something far beyond what his words could convey. "You can own only that which exists in this cave! But you know nothing of that which does not exist, do you? Is that not why you called Me?"

"It seems to me", said Tuko after swallowing several frogs, "that what exists is already so very much too much to bear and to live with that there is little room for what may not exist. What are you talking about?"

"You are still trapped by your culture, by your body and by your idea of what is time, into thinking you know something of reality! Your 'science' thinks it knows about the universe, about viruses, about the brain, about animals. But they don't! It is all an illusion! Everything humans believe is but an illusion. Humans think the universe is an explosion! Hahahahaha! You even think viruses are your enemies, out to get you! Hahahaha! And you believe your brain and your 'logic' give you a sense of actual reality when really they only mirror and reflect your naive assumptions and your egotistical prejudices. This cave will destroy all of your illusions! You think the light is better than darkness. But the cave reveals all the things you see in the light as unreal and leads you through the darkness towards truths that are well beyond the small section of the human brain you are so proud to be aware of. Only when you use *all* of your consciousness can you become aware of what the cave really is! But to 'own' the cave you would need to get entirely beyond the illusion of time and of your limited self."

"How come," Tuko spoke out loud, "that humans are so completely unaware of who they are and of reality, when other animals are not?"

"Now this is the first actually intelligent question you have asked me", came the response and a smile that was almost that of his grandfather.

"If you really want to tap into your full potential, you must use all that nature has provided to you for that purpose. To rely on your conditioned mind, even if you're exceedingly smart and 'scientific', is one-dimensional and quite the wrong path when exploring those dimensions of the human potential you have never experienced. Any merely intellectual approach to absolute Truth is bound to fail. We need to be *also* the body at all times! This is so because mind and body are really the same thing, a Oneness you have artificially divided into a kaleidoscope of conflicting dualities. There are more neurons in your gut than in your brain anyway, and they are more reliable as they are not programmed and brainwashed like your entire frontal cortex! To be really smart, you don't intellectualize! A high IQ means only that your logic is dominant, but it says nothing about most of your *actual* intelligence! Actual intelligence is to use your intuition, your connections to subconscious cosmic knowledge, your body, your instincts and *all* of your senses. To do this, you must find neurological/mental pathways into the centre and the back of your brain where these faculties lie dormant! Humans use only some of their brains because they are almost purely mental, obsessed with their logic, their so-called reason, which none of them even vaguely master, yet cling to as an all there is. You need to use all of your brain, all of your gut, all of your body parts. Which you don't! You train your children to *not* use the body, but to placidly sit by a desk all day! You teach them to use only the eye and the ear for learning, ignoring smell, taste, touch, instinct and intuition! You teach them *nothing* of what is basic and fundamental in life, like how to breathe and eat. You don't teach about sex, death, growing up, about values. Instead you brainwash your children with your patriotic versions of history, with exceedingly nonsensical religions, and cultural traditions and conformities! Why do you teach children to become copies of your own frightened mortal selves? You take away play and self-determination and spoil their joy, including the joy of learning! You respect your children as little as you respect animals, plants and yourselves! They develop into mental and decadent beings that are inferior to most other animals. Which is not saying much. Animals can fly better, swim better, run better, socialize better, build better, sing better, parent better, sense better, and they are One mind/body that is happier, and generally more intelligent, if the ability to survive without destroying their environment is any measure of intelligence. Animals are closer to the truth since they never lie and have never divorced themselves from their bodies or from what exists outside their bodies. They teach their young what they really need, not more, not less. The reason why humans cannot see what great teachers animals are is, apart from their arrogance, their utter inability to perceive from their very limited perspective the truths and dimensions animals take for granted! As a potential, humans have those same faculties, only they pay them no attention and ignore and suffocate them in small children. If human children were raised to use at least the six senses humans are marginally aware of instead of only two, their learning would not only triple, but become multidimensional and non-linear. It would make a huge difference to your evolution...If children were allowed to learn while active, while playing, while learning with their bodies – they would not grow into stiff and divided adults. There are many effective ways to restore children's natural abilities, say to smell almost as well as a dog, to read people as well as a dog, to find intuitive solutions, to become a conscious dreamer, to use breathing like a tool, to become aware of how to use new spaces of the brain by building neurological pathways there, like railway tracks, via attention. If children were allowed to learn from nature, instead of being force-fed your own misconceptions, their intelligence would bring a quantum jump of evolution where humans could actually figure out those obvious questions, like who they are, where they came from, how they relate to the universe and how to not go extinct. Happiness then is a by-product of knowing yourself, having purpose and orientation, and feeling completely connected with all there is. What else is there?..."

Nature has all the answers. Answers are therefore the easiest thing to find. The only difficulty is to ask the right questions! Humans never ask the relevant questions! Their questions are so packed with assumptions, with arrogance and with division that the answers are of course equally useless..."

"That makes schooling completely useless, doesn't it?" Tuko shrugged with the hopelessness of it all. "Utterly useless", whispered the ancient man. "And counterproductive in the extreme! At least the schooling as you know it. Where the body sits still and all the senses are ignored, except for listening and looking, the two senses which are required for your state to indoctrinate you, but which are themselves never properly developed either. Children never learn to become even rudimentary listeners or tolerable observers. And they sure never figure out that smell, touch and taste, as well as silence, humility and awe are also tools for learning."

"So you then think that science is a useless discipline without any merit?" "I don't 'think' this. I observe it! Science, where it is a search for truth and is not built on assumption, tradition or commercial profit, is a good thing. But where do you find such science? In physics, where the acceleration of 'particles' is supposed to give you a clue on what the universe is and how it works? In medicine, where body and mind are divorced and industrial chemistry deemed the sole method for healing? And where viruses and bacteria are an enemy that needs to be 'eliminated' by pharmaceuticals? That is not truth-seeking! It is profit-seeking based on the illusions of division!"

"But haven't vaccines proved to save lives in the past?", said Tuko, not quite ready to discard all that he had been made to believe since his oral vaccination against polio.

"Natural vaccines, like bee stings, yes. But pharmaceutical vaccines only ever work short term, while in the long run they create immunity gaps that weaken the immune system and lead to dependency on ever more pharmaceutical drugs. Furthermore, vaccines aim to fool the prime directive of nature, which is the selection of the fittest, which drives evolution itself."

"And physics? Is everything wrong that physics says about reality?"

"Not wrong. Just useless! Inconclusive! Irrelevant! Narrow and small-minded!"

"So, do you agree that the universe is a living thing? An unborn embryo?"

"Do you really need me or anybody to agree with an absolute and inevitable truth for it to be really true? Do you not trust the One? Or do you believe you alone own the truth, as you own this cave?"

Dancing with the dead

Tuko closed his eyes, rubbed them, and thought about the unsettling words of the old shaman who sounded so much like his Opa, his granddad that had died when he, Tuko, was fourteen. When he opened his eyes again, he sat alone, and there was nobody, except for a little lizard that looked up at him and then scurried off to disappear in an invisible crack in the darkness of the cave wall.

He pondered those words while drinking from one of the places where clean water ran down the cave walls and concluded that his talk with the likely imaginary shaman was about humility and about completeness. He was still incomplete! He lacked humility! He did not own this cave, of course not! He had not even explored its true depth or all of its possibilities. He decided to walk deeper down into the yet unknown parts of the cave, into the very guts of reality. To get to the bottom of things. To the very bottom of himself.

It was completely dark, now, but his feet were confident of their steps and somehow knew where to place themselves. The walking seemed to bring on the mushrooms, and with that feeling the air again took on a fragrance of frankincense and myrrh that seemed to come from the depth of the cave. His movements instantly became very conscious, very dedicated to the here and now. Walking slowly forward into the unknown became a ritual, a dance almost, and he was yet again the High Priest who, for all the rest of humanity, went where maybe no one had gone before. The cooler air deeper down made him aware of still being entirely naked, but his body temperature adjusted with that awareness and he was quite comfortable.

The path narrowed a little and then opened up into a new chamber. He could feel this from the air, quite without needing to see, but as he started to explore, vision added itself to his inner sense and he began to make out structures at the center of the open space. On a rock platform lay a number of little coffins, one of them open, with the lid askew. On another sat the old shaman, grinning like a demon, with one leg over the other, nurturing a look of jovial and utmost relaxed comfort.

"You think I'm not real, do you? That you invented or hallucinated me? Because there is only one reality! One time! Bawahahahaha! Bawahahahaha! Welcome to the dead! It took you some time to get here, but here you are now! Finally you have arrived!" He grinned wickedly and added –"may I introduce you to the real owners of this cave? Or do you prefer to hallucinate something else? Bawahahahaha!

"Here, have a look", the ancient shaman said quite casually, while playing with what looked like a bone that could have been a femur. "These are all children, don't be afraid! They like you! They have accepted you!" He took another bone out of the open coffin, waved it at Tuko, as if to invite him to step closer. " This is Mahal! She was eight years old when she died from the coughing disease. Now she lives here and listens to my stories and dances when I sing. She is quite the dancer. Here, have a closer look!"

Tuko stepped to the little coffin and looked inside, where the remaining bones were laid out in an almost graceful order, as if arranged by something other than time and decay, one finger pointing or curling in a beckoning position right at where Tuko stood.

"Say hello, or she may think you impolite! You never know what the dead see as impolite; they're quite sensitive about these things! Bawahahahaha! And if you think you are imagining her– please touch her to check if she is real! Say hello to Mahal!"

Tuko touched her skull and tentatively said "hello". She was real alright! As real as anything he had ever touched. He thought he saw the skeleton move slightly under his touch, just a tiny wriggle, but this might have been his imagination or else a matter of instability caused by the still connected spinal column. He was then introduced to all the other little inhabitants of the cave by name and told about the illnesses that had sent them here.

" This here is Corazon! She says you can sit on her coffin. She likes you and wants you to be close and comfortable! Here, sit!"

Tuko obeyed the old man and the dead girl and sat. Again, he became aware of a waft of frankincense that was now particularly thick and transported him more and more toward a sense of increased reality where time ceased to exist and space mixed and mingled in rising and falling waves.

"If you still feel insufficiently humble", remarked the old man, "you can ask the children to play with you! That helps! Or maybe you'd prefer to dance with them? They like that a lot! They may even invite you to stay with them for a few years or longer, if you are good at it!"

Strangely, Tuko felt as if surrounded by living children, oblivious of their deaths and prepared to dance joyfully. He saw the shaman move his arms, almost imperceptibly but with infinite grace, and allowed his own body to join and weave in tiny motions, swaying in a rhythm he had never felt before. The dead children seemed more awake by now, their happiness given life by the dance they appeared to participate in ever so gently. The shaman used the leg bone he held to produce a soft beat on the wooden coffin he sat on and tapped a foot against the cave floor in a counter-beat that put even more life into this rock concert of the dead. The air smelled strongly sacred, thick with the mutual embrace of life and death and sweet with the palpable joy of the dead children whose shadows seemed to dance over the coffins and the parts of the cave walls that could be discerned. If any time went by, it could not be measured. If any of the dancing dead was unreal, it could not be detected. There was only a sense of the most intense reality and a music that was from another world but audible in this realm and participated in by the cave itself.

Death itself is what is not real, only life is, mused Tuko, *and reality is not defined by others or by a so-called 'objectivity'. Everything that arises from respect, from commitment and from love is real! Everything that comes with calm and slow breathing is real.*

He closed his eyes and felt the joy of the children as his own, their death as his own and their dancing as a ritual of everlasting life. He felt the gratitude of the dead and he felt his own gratitude as the greatest gift he had received in all of his lives.

"Thank you", he said to the old shaman–but there was nobody there. The music had ended. No shadows danced. Everything was still, as he sat alone among the little coffins, looking at the bone that now lay motionless on the lid of the abandoned wooden box. The dance had ended.

Memories of the future

The air was fresh and new and mint-like when he stood up, and there was a new sense of completeness, a feeling of having lost something unnecessary and gained something precious and unexpected. Death was no longer a far-away threat, but a necessary and even delicious part of him, a piece of the puzzle that gave new substance to life itself. He left the chamber of the dead children and walked on, ever deeper into the intestines of the earth, trusting his feet and his breathing would find the path .

While slowly walking into the unknown he felt no longer alone. It was as if the dead children guided his every step, wanting him to be safe and well. He was thinking of having his own children some day. In his mind's eye he saw a blonde little girl with brown eyes, feisty and full of life, and a tall girl with brown hair, her older sister. Was that a fantasy, he wondered, or a glimpse of the future? He saw the girls climbing trees, playing on golden beaches, splashing around in blue water. The older one was sitting on his lap while learning to play his guitar and then she was playing chess, easily finding difficult solutions to checkmate his king. He saw them sick with high fever and himself wiping their sweat with vinegar, fanning cool air and praying to various Gods to make them well. They were singing together, traveling together, doing martial arts. He loved them beyond anything he had ever felt. He was ready to give his life for them at any time. His understanding of himself was about being a father first, second and last. He walked on, filled with a love that carried his heart and made him feel as if flying over high mountains while he slowly descended into a darkness that beckoned with a warm light of infinite trust and a sense of eternal goodness. He held them as babies, close to his heart, carried them past shadows, careful to make them feel safe and protected and lifted up towards all those wondrous things that could support and guide them and strengthen their paths into a future full of joy. Being a father felt like the quint-essence of who he was and wanted to be. They were his life!

Tuko came to a narrow ledge where the cave floor fell away into the depth, and followed it around a bend to the left that brought him to another open space where water fell from the ceiling and collected in a sizeable pool near the center of the chamber, with smooth, large boulders holding it all together in a basin like an expensive billionaire's swimming pool.

The air was rich with things that lived around water and had never seen sunlight. It smelled of things that happened long, long ago, and it smelled of things to come.

Medicine

The babies were gone. Back to the future. Without further thought, Tuko climbed into the rock pool, which was at one end just deep enough to sit in as if in a hot tub. The water was cool, but not too much so. It might have been old memories of his Opa telling him of the healing powers of water and Kneipp baths and dew-treading in early morning grass–but he also directly felt the healing power of this water as an undeniable reality. This was holy water, alright! It cleansed and sucked all the redundant energies and stale thoughts right out of him, connected him to the outside with its intimate touch, and embraced him with an almost sexual cloak of wholeness. No kind of illness could possibly have survived this physical and emotional purification.

Why are these things not taught at Med School, Tuko wondered, *and why do most people never discover this? Is it not obvious, what a miracle cure water can be? And that healing the body always requires a healing of the soul? Why do medical doctors divide the well-being of the body from the well-being of mind? Why can they only think of chemical solutions? Pharmaceutical companies dictating their training and their world views? How can humans possibly fail to recognize the most obvious truth–that nature provides each and every cure needed for free and so easily accessible?*

Water was magic! It was what humans were made of, what created life in every beginning, and what keeps creating and preserving life always. He drank a few mouthfuls and tasted this nectar of life with his lips, tongue, mouth, throat and stomach more intensely than he had ever tasted anything. He felt immensely grateful.

How can medical science not realize that gratitude is the ultimate healer? That love and laughter and gratitude are the best medicines?

He remembered how his Opa cured his heart issues by discarding the pharmaceuticals from the doctor and taking only hawthorn and garlic and a mouthful of extra virgin olive oil before meals. He saw his physical problem as an emotional one, addressed it as such, and never had any more problems after that! When Tuko had the flu as a child, his grandparents told him that only people who were afraid of the flu would get it and that in their family nobody ever got the flu because they weren't afraid of it. It had certainly worked for Tuko, who never caught the flu again after this. It was all in the mind! All disease was like that.

Maybe, intuitively, he had always known that. When he had found a hawk with a broken wing as a boy, and picked it up with his bare hands, and brought it home, hand-feeding it, touching and stroking his damaged wing while wanting it to be whole again—he had succeeded in getting the bird to trust him, to get well again, and eventually to fly away, visiting for a while before being gone eventually. Similarly, he had kept an injured pigeon alive when he was only seven years old and had no idea what he was doing. Love and positive thought was all he had needed. *Body follows mind...*

Thoughts drifting away, Tuko allowed the holy water to do all the work that needed to be done. It was like he was becoming water himself, or a pebble peacefully resting in a pond of clear, still water. He felt blessed! Unborn. Timeless. he felt the surrounding rock. The cave. No longer human...

He splashed with his hands, breaking the spell, and enjoyed listening to the sound as it mixed with the other sounds gravity coaxed from the water as it fell from above in a natural luxury shower, creating ripples that lapped up against his nipples as he sat there like a thousand year old part of this drama between rock and water. He was supremely well and supremely whole.

Beyond sex

And then he was suddenly supremely hard! His penis and his nipples were rock hard and sending subtle waves of pleasure out to meet the ripples of the water. He stood up in the pool and felt like an archaic God of Nature, flicking water from his skin, pointing at the falling water at a steep angle–a wild thing, the original archetypal male! He did not feel aroused in the sense of wanting sex or of needing a woman–he rather *was* arousal, was full, complete, needless. The cave itself felt like a giant vagina whose sole purpose was to make love and to solicit ecstasy in anybody who stood up in it to be counted. With an intense taste of acidity from his stomach guiding his senses, he was now a nameless, thoughtless and very powerful original force of creation, a thing that exuded sex simply by being complete. To say that he was turned on by his own body was to deny the sheer immensity of the elemental power that expanded in rippled waves throughout the utterly feminine darkness of the surrounding cave. Like his penis, his entire body pulsed with fullness, his leg muscles plumb and heavy with un-spilling sexuality. Like Neptune, his spear ruled the waters of this world, the oceans that pounded to death any mortal man and reserved their life-giving gifts for the Gods alone. He stood under the water where it fell from the sky, his back and shoulders receptacles of all the female power in the universe, as it spilled itself into him, slowing down a stellar explosion into a sustained nuclear reaction that promised to last forever.

Aching shudders seemed to ripple throughout the vastness, pulsing like the archetypal Feminine, a force rarely elicited and never controlled, yet omnipresent throughout the universe. A force only limitless courage could face and live. Water ran freely along the wet walls of the cave, sparkling and playful, yet inexorable, demanding and unstoppable. There was light inside the darkness, laughter mixed with agony, life perpetually springing from death. Time had completely ceased to exist. Thick droplets of joy and rivulets of exquisite pleasure running between the rocky thighs of the great cave, each one carrying the eerie light of a magic that for millions of years had enchanted this place with the enticing possibilities of life.

Peace itself descended with the water and became a baptism that opened his skull and shone like a blue light that only divine gratitude could hope to bear. A deep sense of humility came over him and transformed his towering masculinity into something new, something no thoughts or words could fathom, no mortal could expect to behold. A mingling of divine energies on the other side of ego and of what could be comprehended. A bliss without precedent or reference to anything known or knowable.

He bowed his head, then drank from the holy water. Then he dived and lay on the bottom of the pool, needless of breathing, still like a pebble, immersed in a universe of endless bliss and grateful oblivion. He lay there for a long, timeless time. Then he emerged.

The Sacred

Tuko, raised on the rituals of Catholicism, knew what sacredness was to other people. Something mysterious, the 'holy communion', the name of their God—things that nobody experienced any substance of. When he was a small boy he had considered the forest as sacred, especially one very old tree hidden in a remote and forlorn place he'd discovered and often visited. He'd told this old, gnarly tree, (the botanists had called it an oak), about things only his grandfather would have understood, and only barely. He'd talked to this tree about who he thought he was, about God, about life and death, and the tree had understood because Tuko had a strongly-felt humility towards it–a sentiment he rarely experienced around humans. This humility was the secret to what was sacred and it influenced the way in which he could so intimately relate to the tree and to his innermost self.

Now, the sacredness he felt was absolute! It included all of life, all of his environment, all of himself. It was what lay at the core of reality! It was the underlying principle, the magic, of everything that was and of what was not. It made his heart sing. It combined a quality of serious awe with the abandonment of laughter. It brought out the divine essence in the simplest things and it transformed the illusions of sensual perception into the loudly silent truths of eternity.

Alone the sense of smell could, to a degree, convey the sacred, which was why the religions had appropriated the use of frankincense and myrrh. This same fragrance lay now over the silent drama that unfolded itself in an everlasting moment, carrying and pervading every pebble, every rock, and each of the droplets of holy water that sprayed itself into the world. This holy fragrance did no longer come and go but was simply at the core of Creation and intensified or waned depending on how conscious the beholder was of the magic of it and how in awe.

It changed the way breathing worked. There was an extraordinary receptive gratitude at inhalation, when the divine nectar of it entered the human soul along with the lungs, and filled everything up with golden glory. And there was the generosity and trust of giving everything held precious back to the universe, while all the body cells quivered with joy as the delicious prana distributed itself and worked its magic by penetrating every part of them like batteries storing up goodness itself.

Gratitude made conscious the difference between the ordinary and the sacred, and gratitude came with the humility that recognized the unspeakably precious and the gloriously divine in the simplest of things.

Only the simple things, like water, had this magnificence, this perfect glory, this immaculate wholeness that smelled of immortality. Trees were like that. And so were, Tuko remembered, the hands of his grandmother when they planted a tree in the garden or lay cooling on his forehead when he had a fever. An autumn leaf falling with a splash of color until it lay on the forest floor. The smile of a baby. Things too transitory to grasp, too temporary to belong. The sacred was everywhere, but it was always a thing of the moment, never held or owned or even noticed by the fast and buzzing world.

Tuko sure noticed it now! And, knowing he could never hold on to it, he submitted and bowed to it, trusting to always be a part of this magic.

The Mother

It was then that he noticed a little green lizard as it disappeared into a low, narrow tunnel he had not previously seen. *Coincidences do not exist*, thought he, taking this as a sign to continue his exploration instead of lingering in the eternal moment. He only just fit into the opening and could not see anything. No light at the end of the tunnel. But he had trust and followed the lizard, crawling on all fours on his belly. The narrow space became even more confined until he could barely move. *Should I go back?* he thought, but his trust was strong and so he wriggled onward until he was too stuck to move his limbs or lift his head by more than a hand's width. *Time to panic*, said his brain, but he stayed calm, breathing steadily and deeply. His naked skin did not take too well to being scraped by the uneven floor and being wet did not help. The walls of the surrounding rock were warm, but they seemed to press against him, trying either to push him along or else to smother and squash him to death with their incredible weight. Water trickled. The air was heavy. His death was a near certainty. Nobody would ever find him here. But what was death other than another transformation? A moment of rest? An illusion designed to distract from enduring bliss? Fair payment for what he had been granted?

But there was no rest! The walls definitely pressed down on him in the absolute darkness! Like the powerful thighs of Kali they held him immobile in what increasingly felt like a birth canal and wiped out rational thought in favor of elemental embryonic instinct. Fear and panic threatened to catch up with him now, threatened to convince him to just lie still and die, but there was still this sense of goodness, of trust and of life still waiting for him. He would wriggle as long as he could, lift his head as long as it was possible. He managed to get one fumbling hand ahead of his head, clawing into the rocky floor and pulling himself forward by a few inches. The night and its monsters helped with it and the cave itself pushed and convulsed gently, nudging him forward another inch. His toes dug in and pushed and then his left hand came to a ledge that he used to pull himself forward until his head came free of an opening. He was on a slight downward slope now, and finally came free of the narrow confines and found himself in another space, another world. His hands found a smoothly polished rock, held onto it and then he took a deep breath of fresh air and collapsed.

The Great Mother gives birth to the universe. The Embryo slides from the Inside to the Outside and becomes Man. And God. The waters have broken. Life is new. Everything is good. She is other than the universe, but the universe is still of Her. There is only the Mother. Nothing else exists. She is the source of nothingness and She is everything. She is the cosmic form from which all known forms arise. She is the archetypal first move, that which was before the universe began. She is the embracing universe that surrounds everything. The difference between evolution and genetic reproduction is the difference between an observer contemplating the reproduction of form from inside or from outside the form. She is the 'morphogenetic field' that ordered the Big Bang and all forms inside the universe. She is the One in whose image humans are made. She is the One behind the countless sightings of a woman floating in the air and speaking to the people in Fatima and Lourdes, the Mother of God who works all of the miracles. She is the cause, the reason, the Alpha and the Omega.

He was man and God and newborn child all at once, but Tuko's love for the Mother transcended all he was and was not. His tears ran freely and they were both of unlimited joy over the purpose in everything and of deep sorrow for the blindness of man and his errant science that saw nothing but later 'steps' and disconnected context. They were for the solitude that came from his inability to share the Truth with another human soul and for the end of all solitude that arose from the end of all division and from being a part of the living One and All.

He cried for all the tears he had never shed trying to be 'strong' and he cried for all those whose tears were wasted in self-pity and in desperation, letting his own holy water wash away all the pains of yesterday and clear his eyes for the joy and the beauty he had denied himself throughout all his lifetimes full of fear and separation. And then, after a timeless time of crying, he was done! There were no more tears. Only a little green lizard that fearlessly licked the salty moisture where they had fallen on the polished stone that looked and felt almost like a female breast generously lent to him by a cave the sacred water had carved out of solid rock over millions of cycles. He laughed out loud and the lizard looked at him as if slightly worried about his mental state.

The air should have smelled stale this far down, but it actually tasted wonderful, with a touch of his personal mother in it, as he remembered it from his time as a baby. It also smelled of the potential of ten thousand possibilities and of what life could do if left to its own devices. Somewhat alike to sandalwood. And there was always that background fragrance of Frankincense.

As he looked around, he could see quite clearly the large chamber he was in. He did not immediately recognize any features, as to him his surroundings were much like all there was and could be–a world to look at from large unknowing eyes. But somehow he felt this world full to the brim with Mother, with her smell and her presence filling every nook and cranny and spilling forth from a thousand little oozing drops of delicious juices as they appeared and followed their own secret pathways along the walls of the place. Mysterious drawings and faded paint seemed to appear for moments, telling of things no human mind could understand, and vanished into an absence that itself was the beginning of new narratives and symbols that existed only to again draw his attention to something he could not fathom. The mysteries of the universe itself were laid out and discussed by the faintest hints, by cosmic signs and signals that, like fireflies, existed only for as long as it took to miss their existence in the afterglow of nothingness. But there was not any need to understand, as he contemplated rather than looked, and felt safe, held, reunited and guided by the Unknowable that was the Mother of all things.

And then, while still staring at the near-images and almost-clues of the cave wall, it all came together. Her Face appeared during the blink of an eye, wavered like the weather-tainted signal of a satellite transmission, and stabilized. It was instantly clear to Tuko who he was looking at as his entire body and mind reacted to the bliss of it and threw him into a never before experienced state that could only be described as rapture. He saw a black woman with curly hair that radiated from Her head like the snake-like rays of a black sun. She smiled without smiling, spoke without sound or word, and moved while being entirely still. Tuko fell forward and touched the floor with his forehead, closing his eyes and yet seeing Her, being touched by Her, knowing nothing but Her, remembering nothing at all of what was before knowing Her Face. There was music and this music was a part of Her, a cosmic symphony, barely auditory but felt by every cell in his body. Even his sense of smell was affected, but he lacked the ability to discern or describe the paradisaical fragrance. Maybe it had a quality of Ylang-Ylang or of wild ginger, or a combination of olfactory aphrodisiacs, but his perspective was an ant's evaluation of a Picasso and he dropped the attempt. It was like smelling all the goodness of a benevolent God and all the sexiness of a cosmic Woman rolled into one and multiplied by the number of all the stars in the sky. He was shaken by it as if hit by the blast wave of an immense explosion, yet quivering with it's erotic quality, and maybe he was crying and laughing, but he did not know for sure. He just sat there on his knees, touching his head to the ground and tried to bear the greatness of what was happening to him. He kneeled there for minutes or for years, he did not know.

Laughter

After a very long time, his senses returned and with them the silence and the smells of the cave and an awareness of his body. What remained was the sacredness and the joy, but both were light, devoid of any seriousness, and the overwhelming awe that had held him in a spell gave way to an inner smile that gentled the waves of his heart and restored his awareness of an individual self. He opened his eyes and there was the tiny green lizard looking at him as if to say—I told you so! Then it disappeared as if it had never been.

Tuko laughed out loud. And when he thought he had laughed enough he found this thought so silly and so funny that he laughed some more and then he couldn't stop laughing. The acoustics inside the chamber must have been extraordinary, because his laughter amplified and multiplied as if the cave itself was infected with it and laughed with him, which was even more funny. Tuko laughed about his own insignificance, about the hilarious beliefs he had held, about the nonsense the world taught as true, about the wisdom of the green lizard, about the sense of humor the cave seemed to have in plenty. He laughed at everything he had ever taken seriously, about not being able to stop laughing, about death. Then he laughed about fear, about pain and about missing his dead grandfather. And when he was through he laughed about it all again and the cave helpfully laughed with him. Bawahahahahahahaha it came back from walls and ceiling, BAWAHAHAHAHAHAHA from the opening behind him and a larger one he had not noticed. It reminded him of being in an Australian rainforest with kookaburras all around him, laughing their feathery asses off at the white boy, which made him laugh even more. Never had he laughed like this before. Only once had he come close. It was when he was night-fishing for eel with the youth group of his fishing club and they had put 2 earth-worms into the beer glass of a fishing mate while he was distracted by a bite. After his return to his drink, he had finished his beer, complaining afterwards of the 'one' worm he had found at the bottom of his glass. They had laughed breathlessly, struggling to but failing to get out the words to explain why...The memory of it led to another fit and he struggled with getting a breath and holding his tummy to handle the pressure build-up. His stomach muscles started to hurt.

Why, on earth, had he been so serious about so many things? About figuring out the origin and purpose of the universe! About love! About the pain his iron-fisted mother had caused him as a boy. About the death of his Opa...All those things that happened again and again, none of them final, yet none of them the drama he had made of them. Not that all those things were a joke, but nothing on earth was so serious that a joke couldn't make it brighter and a lot more comprehensible. He could not think of the Big Bang without laughing at the hidden truth behind this expression. He thought of the little green lizard and the distress a laughing cave might cause the poor soul, but he laughed at how misplaced his compassion might well be if, other than assumed, little green lizards could laugh as well. He visualized the little bastard laughing and laughing in its hidden cranny, holding its gut to prevent himself from being too noisy and spoil all that humans thought they knew about green little lizards. It was simply hilarious! There was, of course, some concern that the unrestrained laughter might cause some crack in a cave wall and lead to an earthquake or a collapse of it all, but the very thought of the cave 'cracking up' made it all much worse and was rather counterproductive.

Tuko sensed how the laughter brought about a metamorphosis in his organs. The liver especially benefited from this shake-up. Old worries and grievings came loose and were expelled. His heart had already been light, but now it was ready to fly. Laughter was indeed the best medicine, but that depended on the kind of laughter. To laugh because a drunk friend stuck the bottle in his eye instead of the mouth was what Austrians called 'Schadenfreude' and did little for one's health. But laughing without losing the sense of the sacred– that was the ultimate elixir! The lungs expelled their toxins the fastest, but what was truly remarkable was what it did to the throat! It seemed to open up, to activate and by doing so it increased understanding! To laugh about a thing while retaining one's awe for it led to a much deeper comprehension, at least if judged by one's own sense of humor.

When it was over, Tuko's stomach muscles hurt as if he'd done three hundred sit-ups, which felt rather healthy, and being content just to sit there with a mighty grin on his face was all he now wanted to do. The cave, too, became quiet, needing a rest, but still stood ready to amplify and respond to whatever he was to offer next. The lizard remained gone, which was good, as the little critter was just too hilarious.

How deep to go?

With a fit of sudden rationality Tuko wondered how deep down this cave might actually go, whether he should find out or return to the entrance. However, the laughter was not far away and quickly he discarded the thought that would have led him away from the moment and from the magic. Had he not always lived in his cave? Were those tiny memories of a *before* real or just figments of his imagination? A past life...And yet...He was not supposed to stay here, was he? He was an explorer, maybe. He was a High Priest of the Mother, certainly, and the only home he really knew was the cave, but...

Was there not something else? Ah, yes–humans! Humans...But there were no living humans in the cave and the humans he might have known would never understand or even vaguely relate to his life here. They lived *outside*! If they were real. If they still existed. He had no idea how long he had lived here. There must have been a beginning, somewhere in the remote past. Too long ago to remember, though. Was there an end? Or was there only the moment, here and now? Surely he had lived here and now for many many years. Or maybe forever...

There was no point to such speculations. All he could do was follow his instinct, his inner guidance, and proceed with living the truth as it unfolded. The opening in the cave wall yawned and beckoned and he walked towards it and once again he entered complete darkness. His head seemed to always know when he was at risk of bumping into the ceiling and his feet always knew the way, and so he went deeper and deeper, smelling the air for additional orientation. Like a bumpy spiral stairway it went down and down until it eventually ended in a dead end. There was no way around, but in one place the air was different and there he climbed over a huge boulder and again the pathless path went down, a little left and then right and down again. He heard gurgling water and soon after was walking in it where the path had become a wet and slimy surface that became a little stream that reached up to his ankles. The ground had also become muddy, and squished between his toes. In some places the water ran beside the path and he could feel moss beneath his feet.

The descent evened out, rose for a while and then opened to another chamber. There seemed to be no ceiling and the air smelled fresher. The ground was still wet, but he found an area where it was dry and quite even. His scraped-up feet needed a break, so he sat, resting his head against a well-shaped ledge in the cave wall. There were a few dozen fireflies high above him, too high to investigate, but they naturally lit up the place enough for him to see without needing to use his inner senses. They were beautiful beyond description and they reminded him of stars as they twinkled on and off, speaking of the *outside*, of a world made of light.

What a marvelous thing light was! It was and was not...It was here and yet far away. It traveled huge distances at unimaginable speed to appear on the other side of reality, where the thing that sent out the light had never been and would never be. That made light a trickster! You could never tell what was real with the light! Light could be so beautiful—but you could never trust it. You could not trust your eyes either, for that very same reason. Not like you could trust smell or taste! Light could not be touched. It was a traveler that could never be met. One could see what humans called the sun and one could suspect a firefly—but in actual reality nobody could see either. Light was a projection, a hide-away for things that would not be seen in their actuality. All those beautiful pictures that claimed to depict reality were really fakes, photo-shopped and broken fragments of the nothingness that was pure light. Light could be corrupted, bent and absorbed by things of actual substance...

Yes, a rainbow was pretty. But was it in any way real? Certainly not. It was a plaything made of water, as it broke light into many pieces to produce an illusion. Water was real, but light was a rather Luciferian delusion. Animals therefore did not like it much. They hid from it. They sought its associated warmth, but hid from its glare. Light did not reveal reality to most of them as it seemed to do for humans, as they relied on far more accurate senses and because it revealed their location. Only those that relied on speed, like hawks or tigers, wanted anything to do with light.

Humans were different. They believed everything the light fooled them with. Their other senses, like taste, smell and even hearing, were so reduced, so underdeveloped, as to be rather useless. There might be a rare fair listener here and there, but nobody could be accused of being an adequate interpreter of smells. Humans relied on their eyes, which were the weakest of all senses. They detected only a small section of the existing spectrum, and even of what they saw they could not be sure of, as every magician knew and every judge who had ever interviewed a witness.

And yet, Tuko mused, *humans were utterly in love with their visual sense and with the light! They ruined the night sky with their satellites and they ruined the night itself with their neon advertisements to a point where darkness could no longer be found! All night, the lights were on and perpetuated the illusions of the eye while making all the other senses redundant.*

Worst of all, the brightest of them saw the light as the guide for spiritual awakening and took the darkness for a symbol of mental dysfunction or ignorance! They had invented a philosophy where darkness stood for 'evil' while the ultimate spiritual achievement was called 'enlightenment'. To be 'enlightened' was to be awake, to see the truth about reality, while demons and devils were supposed to dwell in the darkness of ignorance. Light was 'good' and darkness was 'bad'. Yeah, right...

The truth of things, as it just about always is, was the exact opposite. The light of day presented the world of illusion, the worldly and superficial perspectives where everything needed to be mentally known, confirmed by others and taken pictures of. Everybody believed they all saw the same, unquestionable reality. No, the light was simply too fast for the human mind to be accurately observed. The darkness, on the other hand, was the true spiritual realm, where one had to face the truth of all the senses, including the inner ones, without being distracted by illusion. Darkness was the world of the sacred feminine, of spiritual growth, of inner contemplation and meditation. It was the only place where one could be truly awake! Awake to the sounds of the forest. Awake to dreams of other worlds. Aware of the stars and with them of our place in the universe. Aware of fireflies. Aware of the nature of light!

Light could not even exist without darkness—or be missed. During the day, one could not help but see the many roads others had built to get to their meaningless places of worldly importance. But the night allowed one to find one's own path! The darkness allowed one to be born to new places...Not surprising then that Lucifer, the light-bearer, was the 'devil' of religion, and not surprising at all that spirits were believed to own the night. In order to 'see the light' one had to seek in darkness! In order to be born one had to go through the darkness! Just as one could only learn to live with other humans by learning first to live with one self, so one could only learn to see reality by facing the darkness that alone could awaken the senses.

Darkness was safe. It allowed one to be truly with what was. Existence could not be understood without knowing non-existence. Darkness could not be corrupted. In the darkness of night the truth could not be avoided. Darkness was still and at peace. It treated all the transitory things as equally unimportant. It protected the sacred by keeping it secret. Darkness was the sister of silence and the mother of truth...

Sorcery

It was marvelous, Tuko thought, how reality followed attention. Things were not simply what they were but were created, changed and eliminated by attention! If he focused on light, everything he saw was made of light. When he followed the darkness he discovered the secrets of darkness. And that was true for everything in existence! Reality followed attention and could thus be created and changed by shifting attention. He breathed deeply and decided to follow this insight to its depths and its conclusions.

Pain always got worse when it was concentrated on. He'd had injuries he never noticed until he saw the blood. Then they started to burn. Similarly he remembered that self-pity always intensified the pain. He'd used this insight before, at the dentist, where he had eight fillings done in one sitting, without an injection, while simply not labeling what the drill made him feel as 'pain'. He had called it 'intense energy' instead, and had indeed never suffered the slightest bit of pain. After this experience he had gone through a jawbone surgery after a tooth had broken into pieces during an extraction. For over an hour, he had hummed a song, concentrating on the lyrics–and also felt no pain. But he had never drawn the general conclusion that *all* experience is self-created...

Now, in this cave, he was having that same experience, that same insight. It was his questions that produced all the answers! It was what he focused on that evolved into what then happened! The reason why he was able to tune into the secrets of the universe was his intense curiosity, his readiness to focus his pure attention without the corrupting influence of prejudice, expectation or religious predisposition. Just asking a pure question directly brought about the answers! Similarly, he obviously had created a shaman with the purity of his desire to speak to a human...

Was that it? Was the mind behind the creation of all reality? As it was in sorcery? Was sorcery the art of totally focusing the mind on what was to be created? No, it was not just focus. It was more than that. Sorcery was about keeping this focus free of division, of doubt. And it was about using will not as a tool of desire or other selfish and thus divisive and powerless endeavors, but in its purest form, as a thing of Oneness! Will was important, but it had to be free of things like fear, worry, hope or ambition for it to work! Just 'wanting' human company was not pure will, only an inability to embrace solitude and self-responsibility. One had to know that it was right and helpful to have human company; one had to transcend needing and then ask the universe to provide! It was like prayer, really. To pray for a fortune or a lotto win would never work if the desire behind it is selfish, unrelated to real need, and stained with doubt and emotional ambiguity. But praying to the Mother to thank Her for all the wealth and fortune already experienced–that would increase the blessings and might very well, as a side effect, lead to a lotto win! The success of praying, and of sorcery, if there was at all any difference, depended on a technique that required pure will combined with selfless gratitude based on transcended desire.

On top of having pure will and the right attitude, sorcery required a trinity of things. Thought, emotion and ritual! It was quite obvious, really. First, one had to be very clear about formulating a thought. Visualizing an image would do this nicely. Then one had to fill this thought with powerful emotional content that was more than mere desire. And then one had to DO what this thought described and the emotion brought to life, by adding a ritual that closely connected with the thought and the emotion! This could even work in negative ways as in the black magic of voodoo, where first an image was created (a doll), which was then filled up with the emotion of hatred, and finally, in order for it to work, the loaded image needed to be exposed to the ritual of being pierced by a needle...

Tuko remembered when his mother had had what she later thought of as a small heart attack while being alone in the house with him when he was about nine years old. Yes, he had been scared initially. But then, as he prayed to his childhood God while massaging her cramping left arm, he had been full of trust and the belief that he could help her. It had worked like a spell! She had been okay minutes after his intervention. Clarity of intent, powerful emotion, plus ritual...

The scientist in Tuko now wanted to verify this insight and decided to call for the green little lizard or one of its friends. He visualized the little spirit, sent love and admiration, and massaged his thumb for a ritual. Nothing happened...He supposed that rubbing a thumb did not connect with the image or the emotion and tried to think of a better ritual that would. He visualized, loaded the emotion, and drew the shape of the lizard on the cave floor with his index finger, giving attention to detail. Nothing. He let it go and took a deep breath. And there—a mottled brown lizard scurried across the floor right there in front of him, looking at Tuko, and was gone! He wondered what had happened to the green color, but realized that his ritual of drawing a lizard had only confirmed shape but not color. It wasn't so easy to get it just right. One had to line up all of the ingredients or else random influences would fill in for the undetermined or under-determined quantum detail.

Wasn't sorcery then quite a normal part of everyday life? How about all those people who had a dream and later realized just that dream? Those who wanted to become a tycoon, for example, did need firstly a business plan, then the emotion, like strong need and belief in themselves or in their plan, and then they needed a ritual, like working hard every day, to see their plan go to fruition. Was this kind of magic not also what made the difference between guys who were successful with the girls as opposed to those who were not? They had an image of the girl they picked, allowed themselves to feel strongly about that girl, and then went through a ritual, which could be anything from giving flowers to having dinners or rubbing sun-lotion on her body! The better their ritual fitted the image and the emotion–the greater the success. Yes, this was exactly how sorcery and magic worked! Tuko was not really interested in becoming a sorcerer, though. He wanted no power over others. But to have power over one's own beneficial creations was a different thing. He could use magic to develop superhuman powers, couldn't he? Or to improve on his personal development, generally! There was nothing wrong with finding the right rituals for making a good dream come true, was there?

What then was the best magic to develop one's self? Firstly, he mused, one had to discover what abilities were most worthwhile, in what direction to walk. The problem here was that one could not know and judge these things before one had them. But there were criteria here that intuition alone could pin down as useful stepping stones! While it was unclear whether telepathy or telekinesis were worthwhile goals, it was quite intuitive that Oneness, non-division, connection, and selflessness led to a cultivation of the soul in their eventual conclusion. Any real growth mostly required overcoming the divisive ego! Also, it was clear that fear, anger or worry distracted from sober and clear thinking. It was obvious that illusions of any kind needed to be recognized and overcome if one intended to discover actual truth. And it could not be doubted that prejudices prevented clarity. So, even without being able to predict or define the final unknowable goal, it was possible to be quite clear about the direction of the path to take. One just needed to know clearly that all things were connected and then become a conscious participant in that fact.

Secondly, one required an unflinching, wholehearted emotional commitment and the courage to face those obstacles. Like the courage it took to face the ego, the fear, the prejudice!

And finally, one needed a ritual that addressed that clarity of path and linked into the courage and into the love of truth such a path required. Such as–going into a cave, alone, at night! Had he not done exactly that? Renounce the comforts of ego and face the fear to walk into the unknown alone, not distracted by others and by the light of day? What a ritual! And what a magical path! Every step he had taken into the darkness had confirmed this path and fed the magic of its sorcery! His illusions were gone, his fear was gone, his divisions eaten up by a cave that was no object, no 'other', no thing one could step back from and be 'other than'. Tuko felt no pride, only gratitude, at this realization, and he knew beyond any doubt that his path was good and that truth had replaced prejudiced speculations and most vain illusions. Magic was no longer a dream, a fairy-tale, or a thing that belonged to other worlds. It was the very essence of life! It no longer depended on caves or magic mushrooms or exotic places. It was all there was and all that could be.

Again, Tuko let go of all his thoughts and concentrated on his breathing. *Clarity. Gratitude. Joy.* Breathing–the ultimate ritual...

Alitaptap

It was a little bit difficult to drink in this place, but he managed to find a horizontal ledge in a wall where water collected on its way down. It tasted somewhat different, less filtered maybe and a touch of moss or other plants to it. He realized just how much he loved water! It was indeed magical! He had never realized this in his past lives...He washed himself and drank some more of the divine substance, thanking the cave for this precious gift.

He investigated the chamber he was in and found it to be large and irregular. Much of the floor was soft with soil or something organic, not rock like all the other chambers and tunnels he had been in. There were several openings that possibly led to other chambers, but some of them were small and ended after a few meters. He followed one of the larger tunnels to a relatively small space that also led to a dead end. There were fireflies on the walls, and the floor was more even and dry and made of good solid stone—so he decided to stay for a while. The green luminescence of the fireflies, which the Filipinos called 'alitaptap', reminded him of the 'burning bushes' of the bible, and of Boracay, where in December, when the alitaptap swarmed around certain bushes in their courting dance, the nights were lit up in a magical display more spectacular than any fireworks. It was easy to imagine the voice of a God speaking directly into one's heart. Here, in this space, the green light was more withheld, but nevertheless sufficed to dispel the darkness enough for the floor to be quite clearly visible. It was enough to enchant the place and to reveal craggy stone walls that held enough shadows and hidden spaces to inspire a sense of intense mystery. In one corner, there were stalactites growing from the higher parts of the ceiling, and the floor below reached up to meet them with massive stalagmites, bathed in an eerie green light.

As the enchantment grew, Tuko could smell wafts of frankincense and myrrh, and something he thought might be alike to musk. Every breath he took filled his body, or his soul if there was any difference, with fragrances of the sacred, transforming his little cave into a chapel of worship. Time contracted into moments of exquisite glory, and space became all that was and could be in all of reality. His breathing seemed to be guided by the fragrances to become very slow and appreciative, a sacred act of divine flow from outside to inside and back to the outside. The fragrances became a divine nectar and breathing was like drinking the elixir of life. Gratitude became overwhelming. Tears began to form.

As he watched the light-bearing spirits in their magical foreplay of sexual union, Tuko gradually left his own world behind and entered that of these light-beings that also lived here, in the same space, but in an entirely different universe of their own. A true parallel universe. He was drawn in to feel the lives and the experiences of individual alitaptaps at the same rate as he let go of his own individual self, his own way of feeling things and of seeing the world. No longer was he identified with being human now, and no longer was he trapped in a human universe.

I am light. I am sexy. I hope you females can see that. I am on and I am off. I have rhythm. My messages are about being and not-being, about existence and non-existence. I am the light and the truth and the path. Follow me! I am the light in the darkness. I am off and I am on. Can you see me? I am right here. I am right now. I am all there is, all that can be. My life matters. Your life matters. On. Off. Let us dance! Can you see me? I am strong and male and happy. I am the light. There is no tomorrow, only now. Come dance with me. I am the light.

Tiny as they were, Tuko could feel the emotions as his own. He felt the desire to mate, the wish to impress, and he discerned the subtlest nuances in the messages as they were sent and received. He realized how there were individual codes and expressions, and he also became increasingly aware of something like a swarm mentality, where each individual took part and was cognizant of the overall pattern, the entire symphony of light as it assembled from its parts. The entire swarm of alitaptaps was self-aware as One, transcending all duality while still functioning as a polar multitude of males and females intent on becoming One by having sex. It was exactly like music, but with ears and eyes all being one and the same.

On and off was the beat, the rhythm. On and off was the basic program of their digital universe, but a multitude of nuances and meanings produced a complexity that was difficult to comprehend. The conversations included topics related to their environment, like temperature, degrees of moisture, amounts of energy and varieties of textures. But most of it was about sex, sublime sex, and about promises the males made about the divinity of it, the metaphysical nature of the union they knew the females dreamed about. It was about the idyllic setting, the urgency and about the romanticism they all felt.

The females chose their male partners very carefully, based on how easy they were to talk to. They initially responded to several males, but eventually chose the one they had responded to most often. Mating was the high time of their lives and they did not rush or were hasty in their choice of partner. They were horny, but not too horny to find their soulmate first. For this, they used an understated response that required only one segment of their bodies to flash, while the hornier males used two. The actual mating was a matter of tantric ecstasy that lasted for many hours and was of such a refined nature that Tuko nearly lost his mind trying to keep up. The swarm mentality of it all made it a group sex event where he could experience the pleasure of all the females as well as that of all the males simultaneously, which lent an entirely new meaning to the word Oneness. Some of the males getting eaten by hungry females did little to lessen their perfect ecstasy, as all they wanted was to serve and to give and to spread their light for all to see, no matter what. It was an orgy of unlimited pleasure, a ritual of divine consciousness for the entire swarm.

A heavy drop of water fell down the nearest stalactite and was received by its opposing stalagmite, its intimate green glow highlighted by the eons that fit into one moment of complete awareness. Tuko came back to himself, emotionally exhausted and drained by the sexual intensity in this parallel alitaptap universe. Or was it coming back to the confinement of individual awareness that was so exhausting? Hard to tell. He still remembered the existence of an opening in the wall from his memories of being a part of the swarm and stood to check it out. He found it immediately, but it was too small to explore and was meaningless for a huge and clumsy creature like himself. He left the alitaptap chamber and looked into one of the other tunnels that opened up from the main chamber.

Death

It was narrow at first, but opened up after a few meters to a sizable room that had a different smell from all the others. Once his senses had adjusted, he saw why: The floor was nearly covered in its entirety by skulls, human skulls, and what seemed like dozens of them. He picked one of them up and it seemed like a normal skull with no archaeological significance and no indication as to injury or cause of death. The other skulls were much the same and he found no kids' skulls. After his voyage into the world of alitaptaps, these human skulls seemed strangely familiar. Tuko was surprised at humans having ever reached this part of the cave though, given that it required access through the tunnel he had found near impossible to navigate. As he looked at the skulls, his attention took him on a familiar voyage. He understood why they had been brought here by humans instead of buried or used for their practical value. They needed to be underground to be out of the sight of those day-time humans who did not want to be reminded of their own deaths, since they defined life as exclusive of death, as something to be clung to while trying to never think of death. The skulls were here for those few who wanted to know *all* of reality, who dared look at *the other side* of things! Here was where the shamans went when they needed guidance from the *other side*, the side that was also a part of the whole. *Death is the destroyer of illusion, the other side of a reality where seeing only the sunny half makes things spiritually incomprehensible. Those who wanted to see the whole picture, the whole truth of things, needed to have access to the opposite of every truth. As man needs woman, left needs right, good needs bad, so life needs death in order to make sense and in order to work and in order to be eternal and thereby comprehensible.* Tuko sat, as he perceived the fullness of what death was. He had intellectually understood these things for a while now, but this here was at a greater depth and physically real to the core of every cell!

How many times have I died? I am death as much as I am life! I am dying now and I am dead already. I am forever dead and I am forever alive. I am one of the dead! All those skulls—they are my brothers! Because I am dying I may live forever!

He must have blinked, because as he now looked at the skulls, the old shaman was sitting on top of the pile, grinning like a bastard and holding a skull by the eye sockets, like a bowling ball. "This here was a very ugly woman who nobody wanted to kiss. A dragon-lady! If you kiss her now, she would be so happy!" He cradled the skull, then held it out for Tuko to do as he had requested. Tuko took the skull, was quite certain that he indeed had just been given a skull, laughed, smiled and then kissed the remaining front teeth. For the blink of an eye, he saw the image of a pretty young woman, then it was gone and only the ancient man remained. Tuko reached out with the skull—and the old shaman took it and put it back to the others.

"So you finally figured it out." He said it as a statement. "You now know a little better who you are. "Maybe even what the cave is? What the cave is doing here in this reality? Do you know how long you have been living in a cave?"

Tuko had absolutely no idea as to how long he had been in this cave. It felt like thousands of years! But that couldn't be true. He remembered past lives. The last memories were something about being in the Philippines. Yes, when he strongly concentrated there were vague memories of being in Manila, in Boracay, on beaches, making love...But it all seemed very unreal and a long, long time ago. Maybe these past lives were in reality just dreams?

He seemed not to need food, which stood in contradiction to having lived here for such a long time. So maybe he was dead! Physically dead. He pinched himself with his finger-nails but felt no pain. He was dead! One of the skulls! Talking to another dead man! He could not remember dying, but that was common. Maybe he died in the birth-tunnel. Maybe he died from snake-bite. There was really no way to discern whether he was dead or alive, but what the hell! There was really no difference, no either/or anyway, was there?

"You have lived in caves for a million of your years!", said the ancient man. "From the beginning of time! And before the beginning of time... You have been born and died countless times over all these millennia, and most of that time you lived in caves. How long in *this* cave I don't know. I don't chop time into smaller and smaller pieces. Almost long enough! Another thousand years maybe?" The old shaman took on the gentle face of his grandfather for a small moment and added - "how long will it take for you to learn the most important thing about magic?" He counted his fingers and concluded "yes, about a thousand years!" Tuko took a breath and asked "what is the most important thing about magic?" "Oh that", the old man mumbled, then looked sharply into Tuko's eye and said with supreme clarity "there is no such thing as coincidence!" He smiled and then—he was gone.

Tuko grounded himself with a breath, bowed to the skulls, thanked them for their gifts, and left the room. Walking like the living and also walking like the dead merged into a kind of floating glide. It felt alien and interesting, and so he floated and entered another of the openings he could see from the main chamber.

Big snake

Immediately, he had a sense of being no longer alone! A smell he did not particularly care for lay thickly in the air and he felt the hair on his arms and legs standing up as if to indicate a hidden threat. Next, he found several meters of shed skin from a massive snake lying there in the middle of the path. The idea of turning back occurred to him, but curiosity kept the upper hand and he moved past the skin and entered a wider space that smelled even stronger of snake. He walked slowly and took care of where he placed his feet while examining the floor as it revealed itself ever so gradually. He could not see any snake, but there were little bones all over the place that he could not identify. This space also was a dead end and Tuko turned to get back out of the foul-smelling pit, when he saw the snake. It was right between him and the exit, lying there on a two meter high ledge, ready it seemed, to fall on him when he passed below! The beast was huge, bigger than any he had seen in Manila Zoo, her head raised and smelling him with her tongue. How on earth was he going to get past a hungry python that made every impression of planning to have him for dinner? To try and walk past her was certain death, not mere symbolism as the skulls had been. What to do? Pick up a rock and thereby signal his fear and intent to fight? Try and run fast enough by her to catch her by surprise? Sorcery! Projecting what image, though? One of being inedible? Invincible? Too large to swallow? And what emotional content? Fearlessness? But what kind of ritual could possibly convey these things?

Tuko remembered a sustained experience he had had with a python at Father Tropa's place in Metro Manila. Father Eleuterio Tropa was the only 'guru', or spiritual leader, the Philippines could boast. He had stayed with him at his mansion at Rizal Ave, the headquarters of the 'Lamplighters', that was part zoo, part museum of curiosities and part living quarters. Father Tropa had a python and Tuko himself had had it draped over his shoulders while Father Tropa's film crew made a doco about the work of the Lamplighter movement. He had also watched the large snake feed on a few occasions when a life chicken was put into the snake's cage. The thing he now quite clearly remembered was the fact that the snake never attacked the chicken while it still fought for its life trying to find a way out. Only when the chicken had finally accepted its fate and resignedly awaited to be taken did the snake calmly take and swallow it. There was no aggression from that python, only the corresponding reaction to the chicken's resignation and surrender. It had been like a peaceful, non-savage agreement between participants that played the roles of predator and consenting victim. Tuko had then concluded that a predator needed the cooperation, even permission of the victim before it would strike.

Tuko was not going to give any such permission. He was not a cooperating victim or any victim of any sort! He cleared his mind of all thought, breathed deeply and stared right at the snake. And the snake stared back! There was power in that stare and the strong suggestion to just let it be, to relax and to let things happen. He did not fight the power of the snake. He projected his own personality, his own power, and told the snake to relax and to be nice. The snake slowly moved forward, down from the ledge and towards him, still staring. Tuko stood his ground, cultivating fearlessness, staring at the snake with quiet power. The snake circled around one of his legs and moved upwards, putting much of its weight on Tuko's body. The suggestion of logic, that this is how being held in a coil started, became nearly overwhelming, but Tuko accepted it and kept the energy friendly and unworried. The snake looked right into his face, tasted his scent with its tongue, and Tuko stared at the snake with the eyes of the dead. *There is no coincidence!* The snake stared for a while longer, and then proceeded with royal dignity and infinite intimacy over his shoulder and back down to earth. Then it disappeared in a hole Tuko had not noticed previously. Yes, he was dead, Tuko thought, but most definitely he also was very much alive! He thanked the snake for its mercy and its understanding, and lost no further time before leaving its space and floating back to the main chamber. He felt very alive indeed. And that was no coincidence!

The magic of plants

Most of the main chamber had soft ground, soil, Tuko assumed, and smelled fertile. His feet liked the feel and so he floated around a bit, the fertility squelching between his toes. Then, suddenly, his foot refused to step down and upon investigating Tuko found a single pale mushroom growing right there in front of him. He kneeled down to contemplate this marvel, sniffed it and touched it repeatedly. A perfect living thing! It smelled like a forest full of fragrances, like all the combined smells of the cave, like the quint-essence of the earth itself. It stood there all alone, a pioneer of its own kind, and spoke of life. Surrounded by the spaces of death, it was unperturbed in its courage and uneaten by whatever supplied the bones in the snake's chamber. It smelled edible, but eating it did not occur to Tuko who was too enthralled by its perfection to consider destroying it. It was life, like the snake and the lizards, only more committed than either to belonging here, right here, in this spot. He suddenly felt an overpowering love for this creature, and as it always was for him with love, deep respect. Love was respect for things, and people, for being just so. He sat and sniffed some more, becoming conscious of its fragrance being the perfect guide to the simple complexity of what the mushroom was. *As above so below,* said the shroom, and Tuko saw the mycelium underground as it connected to places for virtual or potential other shrooms, some of which had grown here in the past and some that would soon exist in the near future. There was a stand-alone sentinel above ground, but an entire network of life underneath, calling illusion to the idea of isolated and unconnected individuality. The vulnerable-looking shroom was in reality immortal, and when eaten, would pop right back out of the ground maybe a finger's width away. An immortal warrior, then! Tuko dove ever deeper into the shroom's world until, like Gulliver, he entered its actual reality despite his size and his spatial and individual confinements. He could now clearly *see* and sense the mycelium, and *knew* the roots of its being. Roots were like what the past was to humans–origin, birth-mother and source of nutrition. But they were also family, social environment, essential nature and immortal soul. They were the actual thing itself and the mushroom above only its face for the world, its temporary expression. Diving into the underground world of the roots was, so Tuko found, just another way to understand life by facing death. Walking the underworld of roots was to understand the life of a plant, just like knowing death enlightened the life of a human to the point of actual understanding. Roots were what plants used to interface with the earth herself, how they were One with the earth, and the human mind was quite capable to learn this from them and do much the same thing!

Tuko stood there with the mushroom, his knees slightly bent so he could feel the energy flowing freely, and concentrated on earth energy entering his feet and rising up through his body when he inhaled. When he tucked his chin in, he could create a kind of vacuum sucking technique between his sacrum and his occipital bones that made the earth energy go up to the top of his head and, on exhale, ran back down the front of his body. It felt like the earth entering his feet and rising in spirals, and when he returned the energy down into the ground it carried with it every tension, every pain, everything he ever held onto. It felt nutritious. It felt like a battery loading earth energy. It was an interplay between life and death, between earth and human, between individuality and immortality. *How much one could learn from every single, if only so small and humble creature...* Tuko thanked the mushroom for its precious gifts, bowed, and sat down beside it, taking another lung-full of its essence. *There is no coincidence,* he thought, feeling sober, enchanted and grateful.

The existence of plants and humans in a shared and interconnected habitat is no coincidence, he playfully theorized, and instantly saw the deepest meaning in this insight without knowing how to express it as scientific thought, however, or even just thought. *Humans could simply not exist without plants. But beyond needing them for sustenance of the body humans also needed them for travel-guides on the path of the soul.*

Plants give humans the gifts of the earth! Humans, who cannot eat earth directly, can eat plants that can eat earth, and thus eat earth in two steps. Plants are how the earth reaches into the center of our cells, and they are the architect earth uses to build the human structure itself.

But apart from bringing the earth into humans, plants also bring us the light! Humans cannot eat or otherwise assimilate light, but plants can! By eating plants, humans are eating the light! Strange, how such obvious and simple truths are still not really understood by humans...Purely mental 'understanding', as practiced by human society, was only the surface. Real understanding included the gratitude, the incredible gratitude for this gift and the personal joy of receiving it. The real understanding, or the insight, that humans are both earth and light, meant so much in practical ways that it changed everything, and it revealed so much about the building-stones of which magic was made.

Plants connect us with the earth and with the light. Earth and light connect and mingle through plants and humans.

In a well-ordered kaleidoscope of detailed fragments, Tuko could see the many kinds of earth magic, of light- or fire magic, and of plant- and animal magic, as they arose from their interconnecting functions.

For every human weakness there was a healing plant for mind and body, and there were plants that showed actual shortcuts to our best potential and to our deepest selves. Thus, plants connected humans to their past and to their destiny.

Looking at the mushroom kept zooming Tuko's vision in to a point where he could enter its alternate reality. All around the entire mushroom, including the mycelium, were myriads of tiny beings, busy with fantastic transmutations between earth and shroom and utterly committed to serve both to the death and to their utmost personal fulfillment. It was so easy to see and comprehend this microcosmic world if one was not trapped by one's own size and one's modern lack of activated senses...*He would never again be trapped in a 'normal' world of such severely limited cognitive ability as to be cut off from microcosmic worlds or be unable to step out of the narrow confines of this contemporary non-perception as an isolated species.*

However, one could lose oneself in those worlds quite easily, and possibly fail to ever return...It was so easy to let go of all personal memory and release oneself utterly into the moment and into forms that are so very different from humans! A weak human, or one that was very unhappy with who he was, might well stay in such worlds and never find their way back or even remember there ever was such a way. No, this was not for everybody. But he was centered enough, aware enough of being both this and that and nothing exclusively. A wanderer. A wanderer who could go there but always retain the choice of whether and when to stay and when to go on.

No, Tuko did not stay in any of the microcosmic worlds, but he bodily stayed with his new friend, the mushroom. Its fragrance was addictive! It built an instant bridge to so many ancient and archaic memories and forged Tuko into one piece with his most ancient past, his ancient past that was old lives, ancestors, evolutionary steps, alien things, monkeys, and the earth itself. It was something known from long ago, then forgotten and found afresh, and now it was like coming home. And the shroom had nowhere to go, nowhere else to be...

A human seed

When Tuko decided there was nowhere to go, he curled himself into a foetal position and lay on the earth beside the mushroom. He folded all he was and all he had ever learned and experienced into himself to contemplate and meditate what he had become. He closed his eyes and yet continued to *see* the shroom and the chamber. He folded them both inside as well and after doing so let go of the *outside* entirely. There was now only the *inside*.

The inside contained all that existed–the shroom, the snake, the alitaptap, the dead, the entire cave, the universe itself. Like a cosmic origami, the inside represented all of existence and like a mango seed knows exactly how to become a mango tree and how it had once been to be a mango tree, he now became a fractal of all that was and could be and would be.

I remember the light and the day of man. I remember the path I took to get here. I remember the illusions, the ambitions, the denials, the fears and the imagined achievements. I remember large open spaces. But now, I am dead to all that. I no longer move or strive. I slumber. I have slumbered for a million years, dreaming of things that are not. Dreaming of things that no longer exist and of things that have never been. I am dead and I am alive. Time no longer exists. I am the speaker for the dead and the voice of the earth. I am the light that glimmers in the greatest depth of eternal darkness. I am invisible to every eye, yet deep down I still dwell, a sleeper throughout the millennia of personal death.

I am the seed from the remote past and the seed of a far away future. I have no hands but I know how to change. I live through the ages because I am dead or mostly so. Who am I? I am nothing anybody can see, yet I am all there is.

I am the mighty sorcerer who can shape and create all of reality and I am enchanted beyond comprehension by the smallest things. I am the power of the earth. There is darkness everywhere and I am the lone star that dimly sparkles when there is no eye to see. I am the human dream of becoming God.

I am the sleeper who may sleep forever, keep all his secrets forever. I dare not whisper of those things long dead, because their silence is sacred and even though only the earth might listen it is not my time or place to speak. Not now. Now belongs to the silence alone. Too deafening is the silence that ended time and swallowed my sincerest whisper.

I lie here in my earthly grave, not grieved for by living things, un-mourned by the future; yet my Mother is holding me in her warm embrace, close to her beating heart, and sings to me her silent lullaby. She pulls her blanket made of darkness and woven through with silent spells over my polished nakedness, tenderly and with so much love.

The dead of ages are my only company, my sole retreat. Sharing my silence, their bones lie still, like me. Their whispers long dispersed, their movements come to peace, their dance of stillness a fleeting and long forgiven memory.

I am the seed of God, wide awake in my deepest slumber. My potential is endless, but my hands are folded and my knees are bent, so I might well fit into my Mother's womb. I know what a God must be, but I hold the secrets tight to my heart where only I can see.

My breath catches the scent of frankincense and other essences that belong to the body of the earth. Intimate smells, too sacred to behold without the gratitude of a God holding them close.

I am a fractal part of the unspeakable truth. The one that holds it all inside until the beginning of time has come. I am the answer to all questions never asked.

I am the seed. My flower has wilted from seeing too much light. My leaves are gone. My roots were lent to me, were never really mine. I am the seed.

One day, so say the tales, I may awaken when kissed just right by the light. A hero may then grow from those forgotten bones, and break the shell that stops him from reaching for that light of day. So say the tales, whose jaded voices are no more than trails of faded memories.

I am not waiting for the light or for the water's nudging touch. I am too fully here and now to speculate about a future that may never be. I am content and entertained enough by listening to the silent songs of millennia that come and pass. But I am wide awake and will not miss the call that one day will pronounce 'the time has come'.

Until then, in my Mother's womb I sleep while time stands very still.

Tuko did not sleep, but he was deep inside himself when the first sound broke the air. An angel's wings? Then more fluttering wings. And before Tuko fully accepted this outside reality, all hell broke loose! The air was filled with the agonized cries of demons, the din so enormous it swallowed all of the sacred silence in the blink of an eye. He sat up and felt something like rain drizzle down on him while the demons boiled the air all around him. He moved under the nearby ledge and pressed himself against the cave wall, trying to avoid the worst of the onslaught. He opened his eyes and saw hundreds of bats, as they entered the cave from an opening that he had thought was a group of fireflies near the ceiling. It had indeed been stars! The multitude of bats continued to flutter for a good while, as they each found a place along the ceiling where they then hung, upside down, after a night's feeding in nearby mango trees.

There was just enough light for Tuko to clearly see the cave entrance, up a forty-five degree rugged incline to where the stars had been. Light! An opening just big enough for a human to easily climb out! No need to return all the way to where far back in the past he had once entered this cave! He stared at the opening, where the light of early morning revealed an actual path to the outside, and tried to get to terms with this new and very unsettling reality.

The path up and out

After thousands of years, there is now light! It tickles the slumbering seed. The beginning of time has arrived! The God within lifts his head in anticipation of a beckoning future. The Mother spreads her legs and feels the Coming of a new day when the soft light kisses her moistening womb and licks her plumply earthy thighs. The long night is nearly over.

The young God's heart will surely burst its confining shell! It longs for the light like the swelling seed and yet...a great longing to stay with the Mother still keeps him firmly rooted in the earth, makes him turn his head... back to where the darkness still has all the magic he knows and where the dead now hold their dance and throw their bones to keep him here.

The cave whispers. The silence has fled. Everything stares at the light, not knowing if it spells the end of it all or, like all death–a new beginning. The voices of the dark call him back. They speak of dangers and seduce him with the sweetness of their long-held embrace. The retreating darkness pulls on him to flee down into the depths of the cave. How sweet would it be to slumber some more, to ripen and swell before leaving Her womb and grow towards the light.

The light, that also pulls, claiming inevitability and purpose, and draws out life from all the most hidden places.

Needing all of his strength, Tuko got to his feet, facing the light and took a hesitant step towards it. Long forgotten memories painted the future in all those colors he had once known and promised the happy songs of birds that would fly up high into a blue unending sky to celebrate that time truly had begun. And yet– the safety of the earth wanted to hold him, warm him and be his home... for eternity. From every nook and crack in the cave walls trickled the intimate fragrances and reached out for his soul to stay.

He took another step, but his legs were short and thick from hesitation and when he turned back one more time he was an old dwarf who knew of treasures hidden in the cave that he wanted to protect and who feared that the greedy day would take them all away by the forgetfulness of hasting time. But now the cave was empty and he alone was its fullness that it pushed before it like a child. He himself was the earth where all the treasures rested, the swelling germ that knew only one direction. His legs were just long enough to take another root-bound step, but now pulled by threads made of gleaming gold he felt his way towards the opening in the great belly, carrying the warmth he had known, and the feeling of a home up with him where, aged a thousand years, he for the first time saw the day, the golden, singing day.

Only a few more steps, and I might step from the earth that still clings like a love-made glue to my feet as if I were a tree that dreaming itself in the highest branches of the sky still drank from its deepest roots.

Stuck between inside and outside, heaven and earth mingled in his body and he felt the sky down to the roots of his very being. He looked down at himself and saw only an egg-like glimmering energy that nearly touched the ground while it floated very slowly towards where those golden threads pulled his heart.

Only a few more steps, and I might step from this cave into a much bigger, wondrous space, sing with the birds of a waiting sky and fly from my egg-like self into blue heights where I might join the fragrances of tropical flowers and where, forever thanking the Mother, I might then glow and surely die in the golden light.

Only a few more steps...

About the Author

Fritz Blackburn, born in Augsburg, Germany, studied law and economics before he traveled the world on a shoe-string and lived in remote cultures. He learned about mind development from Mexican shamans like Maria Sabina and explored the possibilities of the human mind using the peyote cactus and psylocybin mushrooms as well as other techniques that cultivate the human potential. He taught yoga in the Philippines where he ran his own school on Boracay Island.

www.ingramcontent.com/pod-product-compliance
Lightning Source LLC
Chambersburg PA
CBHW031646170726
47990CB00019B/2572